THE THEORY & PRACTICE OF APPARENT LOGIC

APPARENT LOGIC

THE ART OF MAKING COMPELLING ARGUMENTS
WITHOUT THE NECESSARY INGREDIENTS

PETER STEER

Paperback ISBN: 979-8-9988549-0-3

EBook ISBN: 979-8-9988549-1-0

Cover Design by GetCovers
Print Formatting by Vellum

TESTIMONIALS

"This is a dangerous book. The Queen's English was never meant to be bastardized into such an assembly as is put forth by my brother in **Apparent Logic**. The existence of this book calls into question the very foundation of our education system and screams out the existential choice we now face: Really ... should everyone be taught to use words?"

TJ Steer, former F-14 Pilot, former Commercial Airline pilot, my little brother

"This is the most important, unnecessary book of our time. I could go on, but really ... what's the point?"

Titus, flew F-14s with TJ, flies Fed Ex, my friend from school

Apparent Logic looks at the truth and asks, "Can't we do better?"
Peter Steer

"As an early adopter, I became a field researcher and practitioner of Apparent Logic. I am fascinated that this way of thinking and then expressing yourself, or you could say, this way of life, invokes Newton's Third Law. People are strongly attracted to your bold choice to walk the high wire and launch into a story with Apparent Logic, when you didn't really have to. And soon enough, they have an equal but opposite reaction, where they are repelled to a quiet place to let their brains unscramble. This observation will undoubtedly form the basis of master's-level inquiry and curriculum at the Institute."

Bill, grew up on our dead-end street, youngest of 8 boys, knows how to talk fast.

"Most of it is believable ... and some of it is true!"
Peter Steer

"It's the Go-to for the How-to on humorous storytelling"
Mike Gardner, Founder, Outside the Box agency

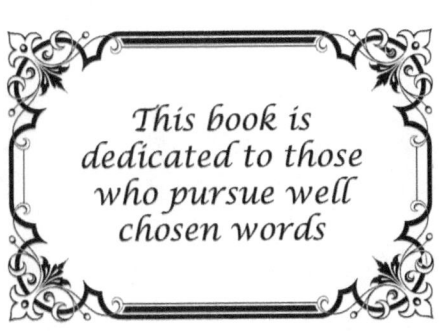

*This book is
dedicated to those
who pursue well
chosen words*

ABOUT THE AUTHOR

Peter Steer is a keen observer of things often overlooked. Fueled by a strong curiosity, he is not content to just leave well enough alone. This is Peter's second book. His first, *Catalytic Thinking*, explains the Creative Process and how to generate breakthrough ideas. So, if you combine the impact of *Apparent Logic*, with *Catalytic Thinking*, and Peter's work in plastics recycling ... he would tell you he is busy making the planet a better place.

Help Peter on his quest by following his work and subscribing to petersteer.substack.com

CONTENTS

CHAPTER I

A HUMBLE TRIBUTE TO A SMALL BOOK WITH A BIG IMPACT

My fellow readers … I first want to remind all of you that we are each one third of a lifespan. One third of the responsibility to pass on wisdom, folklore, family history, and humor of the day. We are all the Child, and hopefully the Parent, and with great fortune we are then the Grandparent. I have had this book in mind for the last ten years, which finds me now at 64 of them. My Dad has recently passed away, and my two boys are in their mid-twenties. Just place yourself somewhere in any of the thirds… you got something from your Dad, which he got from his Dad. That possession percolates within you, and you want to deliver it to your child…because even through three generations, it is timeless and relevant today.

It is a wonderful tapestry, and no two are the same. The fabric of this generational tapestry may be family stories. It may be a cabin or lake house visited for years. It may just be the dining table where so many meals were shared. I have a swivel office chair from my grandfather's office that I reupholstered and varnished the arms myself. Maybe it was a set of tools aptly used by generations of your family. For me, part of that fabric is this beautiful little book, given to me by my Dad. This book carries all the laughs from those who enjoyed it before me.

Gamesmanship is a small, hard cover book by Stephen Potter, and illustrated by Lt. Col. Frank Wilson. Published by Henry Holt and Company in New York in 1952, then republished in 2013 by a charming, small English publishing house called Elliot & Thompson. I look forward to discovering the impetus at Elliot & Thompson behind bringing Potter's work back to life, but I already know the answer. The wisdom and wit in this book are timeless!

The subtitle says it all …

"The Art of Winning Games Without Actually Cheating."

Even if you are not a writer, I want you for a moment to put yourself in the shoes of the person who puts pen to paper. What are the greatest accomplishments you could achieve? There are a few. For a cartoonist (similar dynamics to a writer) it would be to have your drawing chosen to grace the pages of the New Yorker Magazine. The greatest dry wit is found in those pages. I collaborated with my friend's daughter, Charlie, to create and submit an entry we thought worthy of their consideration. Charlie is a fine artist with a brush, and this collaboration was her first cartoon assignment. I think Charlie knocked it out of the park! I consider our cartoon collaboration a masterpiece and while it didn't make it into The New Yorker, it deserves a place in this book.

Here it is:

"Sea Bass... again?"

Can you imagine a hard-working Chilean miner complaining about being served what we consider an absolute delicacy, Chilean Sea Bass, yet again? I think it also pokes fun at us here in the USA who only know Chile for their miners and sea bass. They also make mighty fine wines!

Another career highlight for a writer is to make the best seller list. Well, I fully intend this book to take its place on that list. But there is something higher to achieve, and Stephen Potter achieved it with his groundbreaking tome The Theory and Practice of Gamesmanship. What Potter did is put a word of his own into the lexicon for future generations to come. Gamesmanship is now known the world over because Potter introduced his works at the Institute where Gamesmanship is practiced and honed into craft. That's why his work deserves a tribute.

Consider this ... at any given moment, the number of words we are allotted to conduct our daily affairs ... is finite. God bless those who add a word to this inventory, thus expanding our verbal and written potential as a species!

Having fallen in with a group of golf buddies in my early 20s, it was that tag line that drew my attention to the book. We would always try to gain an advantage over each other by the style (or lack thereof) of our attire, or verbal taunts and other intimidation designed to upset a player. We wouldn't yell in someone's backswing, but we would certainly try to be the thought in their head as they are swinging.

I can't say if this particular gambit was hatched after reading Potter's book, it could have happened well before but either way Potter would have been proud. After relentless, and I hate to admit ... effective taunting by Jocko on the course over the course of a summer, I needed a drastic reply. Someone once said, *"you go to war with the army you have."* So, I borrowed that thinking. Another passion of mine is fishing, and I always had some bait in the freezer of my parent's home, how they allowed that is beyond me.

With an early tee time and only a half hour drive to the course, I was in no jeopardy of giving up the jig by having the frozen mackerel that I grabbed thaw out on the ride and stink up the car. No, it was still frozen when we got there. As we were getting set to play on this hot August day, I took the mackerel out of my golf bag and then out of the bag it was in. A mackerel is a long slender fish, so it fit easily into Jocko's golf bag, coming to rest down ... down by the handles of the clubs.

By the 5th hole, the sun was blaring.
Jocko was not hitting the ball well.
By the 10th hole, his grips were smearing.
Jocko was not swinging his clubs well.
By the 15th hole, his eyes were tearing.
Jocko was not feeling well.
At the 19th hole, his buddy's eyes were tearing ...
from laughing at the successful gambit!

Gamesmanship was on full display that hot August day!

When I was younger, I always had a liking for vintage things, so maybe I paid more attention to the past of the generations that preceded me. I learned golf from my grandfather, with his old leather shoes and heavy golf bag. I took from my parents a love for Burt Bacharach, Dionne Warwick, and Herb Alpert! I believe that vintage clothes are always in style. Now older and having been entrusted with these cherished items, I feel compelled in some way to make them accessible and appealing to the future of the generation following me, including my Nick and John. I hope this tribute to Potter's great work updates and refreshes the style of dry wit humor he doled out effort-lessly and copiously!

Now instead of engaging in a sporting arena where the lack of skills is replaced by fluent Gamesmanship, I offer similar prepared-ness with Apparent Logic, for those brave enough to enter the arena of ideas without the necessary ingredients!

CHAPTER II

THE DEFINITION OF APPARENT LOGIC

I open this chapter with a declaration of "No Bullshit!" because it is too easy to jump to that conclusion at first glance of this book's subtitle. "The Art of Making Compelling Arguments Without the Necessary Ingredients" sure sounds like a bunch of B.S. and not the truth, right? The problem is that until now, if you didn't have the correct answer, then there has not been a recognized verbal path other than a lie. Let's be clear, lies are bad. Lies destroy a part of both people. The liar shreds their own dignity and credibility, things which are very hard to build back. The person lied to is deprived of critical information that would have them make better decisions for themselves. Lies are verbal rot and decay.

Did you know one can only Lie if one knows The Truth? It is a meditated act. I hesitate to use the word "premeditated" because in the thick of it lies fly out without regard to the moral filter that should suppress them, thus causing harm.

Now, with that foundation, let's look at the opposite path ... The Truth or The Correct Answer.

To segue from above ... one can only give an Incorrect Answer if one doesn't know The Correct Answer. That's the difference between a lie and the incorrect answer. Apparent Logic is not an alternative to a lie as it does not come from where lies originate, which is fear of the truth. Apparent Logic comes from the opposite place, which is boredom with the truth. Apparent Logic looks at the truth and asks, "Can't we do better?" Wow, that might qualify as profound.

For purposes of this book, I equate The Correct Answer with The Truth as they are both very important starting points. To give an answer, it would be great to be able to share the Truth, or The Correct answer each time. You would be a walking encyclopedia. But we don't have that luxury. Often, we will know something about where the story is heading but not enough to get off the sidelines and offer your explanation. Silence is also encouraged by fear of your incorrect explanation coming off as a lie.

So now we know the guardrails of The Truth and The Lie. We know the silence from just not trying to fill the in between with some answer, some explanation that will get the listener to the same place. Practitioners of Apparent Logic don't like that silence. Apparent

Logic is the path that lies between truth and lies, just as Gamesmanship is the path between fair play and cheating. That pun was not intended but let's just always be blessed when one shows up! We welcome the brave soul who charges into the void between and offers an explanation that is not completely correct, although the intention was to be completely correct. Think of the lack of necessary information as an invitation to deploy Apparent Logic. We do so, charging into the void knowing, and celebrating that we don't have all the correct information but with the power of well-chosen words we weave together an explanation that gets the listener to the same place of thinking as would an explanation that is completely correct. What a beautiful service to mankind to provide exercise to our brains and the muscles used in laughing.

Apparent Logic does no harm as it is not intended to deceive. Apparent Logic has no malice since its logic is displayed for anyone to pick apart. It is deployed with cards on the table, and perhaps with a "tell" of a wry smile. That smile will soon be shared by all because the words chosen in a good Apparent Logic story are happy words.

What do I mean by happy words?

I don't mean words that are arranged in a manner to make the listener happy. It is not words like *"We appreciate your work so much we are making you a partner in the firm."* Nothing against each of those words, or the arrangement, if you are trying to make the individual in that firm happy. That's not what I mean by happy words.

I mean that the actual words chosen are happy that they are getting called off the bench and put into the arena! Remember, when one gives the Correct answer, those words have been called into action time after time. They are bored with the repetition and have even grown weary of each other. They only slightly perk up on the bench when the host chooses to lie instead, bringing out those bruised, hurtful words. But that is just a sad spectacle with a forgone conclusion.

Ahhh ... but when Apparent Logic words are well chosen, they are thrilled. Each and every word being used delights in participating in an explanation so intricately woven around the scaffolding of truth! The unbridled enthusiasm contained in each word grows as each layer of the story is birthed by the words that preceded it. The energy is visibly felt by the person telling the story and is stage 4 infectious to the people hearing the story!

It is your choice to participate in the verbal or written arena, knowing you are not armed sufficiently. But this is where brave souls must tread. A question not answered, an explanation not given … creates a vacuum. Nature abhors a vacuum, and practitioners of Apparent Logic are those foot soldiers obliging Nature by filling it in!

An Apparent Logic story may be a shortcut to getting people on the same page. Perhaps it is even courteous as to not waste valuable time getting there. The shortcut is from the alternative of researching down to the exact, correct answer. That doesn't mean a dose of Apparent Logic has to be brief in length. An Apparent Logic story can also be a "longcut" that still gets the listener to the conclusion desired. Several of the stories in this book are quite long, so think of all those words made happy when put into play! So, to summarize…

The Correct Answer doesn't care if you accept it
A Lie demands that you believe it
Apparent Logic invites you to follow it

You may be asking yourself, "How do I know when someone is diverting into an Apparent Logic story? How will I recognize it?" Well, it's not like porn, where you can only recognize it when you see it. But maybe it is like porn, where attaching with a hyphen the word "porn" as a modifier to the end of another word that is a noun, is meant to show that the noun is to be considered expressed in the Nth degree. There is a feature in *Wired Magazine* where they honor a visual display of data that is so incredibly spectacular. That feature is called "Infoporn." So Apparent Logic may one day be graced with the description "Story-telling porn." Wait … not porn within the story being told … that's not new nor groundbreaking. Earthshaking perhaps … but I digress.

Here is a way to recognize Apparent Logic in action. The story-teller begins. Perhaps there is an audacious claim at the beginning of the story that gets attention. As the storyteller drops a few facts into the story, if the listeners were to voice their buy-in, they would say *"Yes!"*

Now the storyteller uses those facts as lattice work on which to hang Apparent Logic material that seems a bit shaky. The listeners' buy-in expression at this point in the story would be *"Wait ..."* with a suspicious tone.

This is where the listeners are trying to digest words that have already passed them by. The storyteller cannot be slowed down to wait for comprehension to catch up. No, the storyteller is fueled by the words themselves and the anticipation of opening each next door to where the story goes. Here is where interaction with the listeners may jog the story to work around an exposed flaw. But the story continues hurtling toward its conclusion, leaving no time to readdress the work-around given but mere moments ago. The listeners are too busy catching up, so they don't have time to ponder why they are still listening. The listeners now follow along, very curious to hear how the beginning can ever be squared with the ending.

It is a race now!

The storyteller and the listeners are both in a race, but to different places. The storyteller races to the completion of the Apparent Logic story, to land it without too much more damage to the fuselage. The Listeners race to a level of comprehension that distills all the parts of the story, sorting out what makes sense to them, to where the listener's expression is simply *"What?"* or more like *"WHAT?!"*

The storyteller has taken them full circle. From the initial agreeing nod from the listeners, they arrive at the end of the story a bit roughed up, in a literary sense. You have landed them in a place of agreement in which they haven't gone completely willingly, which can be mildly disconcerting. It can also be greatly rewarding to the listeners, as they may feel as if they survived an exhilarating, yet dangerous, toboggan ride. Who doesn't love that feeling?

I'd say if you see this reaction from listeners, then you have just seen a practitioner enjoying the art of making compelling arguments without the necessary ingredients. You have just been enrolled in The Institute for the Theory and Practice of Apparent Logic. Whenever two or more are gathered in the name of Apparent Logic, then school is in session. Apparent Logic just needs listeners to be smart enough to know the story has parts that are wrong, and tolerant in knowing. But also, not fast enough to stop the story before the teller supports it well enough for the story to move the listener to the point being made by the teller.

It is actually a great skill to be able to recognize something that is wrong. We can't go through life taking things at face value; that is being naïve. Apparent Logic helps hone that self-defense skill. Here is a wonderful story, that may be true. A student took the SAT and scored a perfect zero. Why call it perfect? It was unblemished by a single correct answer. It was perfectly wrong.

Guess what? She got into Harvard! Why? Because the Harvard Admissions team realized the student had to know what every correct answer was, in order to choose a different, incorrect answer! This student was perfect at being wrong! After a life of being wrong plenty myself, I admire this gambit! This student would certainly challenge a great Apparent Logic story in progress so, all you future Apparent Logic practitioners beware and be ready!

As I reviewed this story and was happy with the points it makes, I realize that I used the wrong terminology if my profound statement earlier is to be true. One can only lie if one knows the truth. One can only give an incorrect answer if one doesn't know the correct answer. The biggest difference between an incorrect answer and a lie is how the lie hurts someone. Since she knew the correct answer but marked the wrong answers ... she deceived on purpose. She wasn't incorrect ... she lied. She potentially hurt Harvard by depriving them of accepting a brilliant student, and she hurt herself by potentially ruining her chance to attend such a fine institution of learning. She was lucky they saw through and forgave the lie and accepted her! Had she not, I'm sure she would have fared rather well at The Institute for the Theory and Practice of Apparent Logic!

Perhaps we need a tangible example of Apparent Logic before we dive into the stories that follow. Dare I say the timeless and universal stories of the Tooth Fairy and Santa Claus are the quintessential examples? Let's run them through a few Apparent Logic filters ...

Do those stories hurt anyone?

No. In fact, quite the opposite. These stories are filled with joyful words, producing wonder and excitement.

Are there facts upon which the stories are built?

Well, the tooth is not under the pillow in the morning, and a dollar bill is!

And I did see another kid missing a front tooth, so he will get mine, thanks to the Tooth Fairy. There is a glass of milk that someone drank halfway down, apparently too busy hauling presents to finish the glass. And two of the four cookies are gone!

Now the tree has bunches of wrapped presents that weren't there last night ... and some have my name on it!

And just to bring the realness home ... NORAD is tracking Santa's sleigh across the globe!

Is there preposterousness in the beginning of the story that hooks the listener into the verbal adventure?

The magic of the flying sled and reindeer surely grabs attention. The wonder that the Tooth Fairy will take my tooth right from under the pillow I sleep upon would fill me with such excitement that I would try with all my will not to fall asleep!

We will study these attributes of an Apparent Logic story in Chapter 16 where we tour The Institute for the Theory & Practice of Apparent Logic and glean important ploys and gambits that have been workshopped in the Institute and deployed in the field by the legions of practitioners.

So, let's dive in, shall we?

CHAPTER III

THE THEORY OF FINITE HUMOR

T heories attempt to explain things, and even when they are proven wrong, they still seem to help the original presumption hold some higher level of importance. There is efficiency in apparent logic ... a shortcut, or a short circuit, straight to the intended result. In the same moment that you agree with this theory, you will also feel disconcerted that it was apparent logic that brought you there. A beautiful paradox.

The Theory of Finite Humor maintains that a person's humor is dispensed in a finite amount. Not the same amounts...just a finite amount. That means that each humorous event: a joke, a story, a monologue, or toast has differing amounts of humor, but again I stress that each event's humor content is finite in quantity. Of course, too, is that the finite quantity of humor dispensed, per humorous event, ranges greatly from one individual to another.

So, if you understand those parameters of the Theory of Finite Humor, let's play out what it means. If eleven people are in the room, and one of them offers a joke that all of the others *get*, then each person enjoys their share (or 1/10th) of that finite quantity of humor that was in that person's joke. Keep in mind the two variables that effect that finite quantity are the person delivering the joke and the joke itself. Here's where it gets better. If only two people *got* the joke, then the amount of humor enjoyed by those two was the whole amount divided by two, or 5/10ths each. That's 50% versus the 10% where everyone *gets* it, a five times greater reward for those two recipients than when the humor is shared by all. That's why an inside joke is so powerful!

Now understand that The Theory of Finite Humor applies equally to everyone, but it doesn't make everyone equal in terms of humor. A really successful comedian is just gifted with huge volumes of humor. When Jim Gaffigan or Chris Rock dispenses their jokes, each contains such a great quantity of humor that it doesn't dilute that much amongst the crowd...and they can really light up the room. Compare, in contrast, to Al Gore. A humorous offering by Al, (of course aimed in a non-exclusionary way) would be spread out amongst the entire crowd, barely resulting in a murmur of laughter or a low-level chuckle. Under this Theory of Finite Humor Al would be what's known as quantity-challenged.

The *greats* know about Finite Humor and most practice it fluently. They'll toss out something that they know very few people will *get,* but they also know that those who do will be rewarded with a real treat ... a huge quantity of humor resulting from splitting the pie with fewer people. The recipient's natural response is a tighter allegiance to that comedian ... and as a reward to that comedian, they become a more loyal fan.

Ahhh ... but it is not as simple as this seemingly win-win equation. This is a no-pain-no-gain scenario. The sharp edge of the Theory of Finite Humor is that there is a social cost that increases incrementally with winning each next loyal fan by use of the inside joke. The people who don't *get* it, the people on the *outside* of the inside joke, will eventually look at you funny, eventually lowering their opinion of you. You are basically sacrificing what they might think of you for the greater pleasure of the smaller group that you reached with your inside joke. Strategically, it may be those people you care about while accepting the loss of regard by those left in the dust. Think of it as a culling out process.

To give an example, I submit Andy Kaufman. He was considered by many a comic genius, but those *many* people are definitely a small minority compared to the masses, who thought Andy was a complete ass in his later comic efforts. He obviously traded a huge social cost for the addiction to the praise of his dwindling list of worshippers. Perhaps Andy thought shallow praise is finite in quantity too, for as his fan base plunged like the Nasdaq, he must have felt compelled to draw ever-increasing quantities of praise from that smaller and smaller group ... a recipe for self-destruction. How sad and ironic that during his short battle with lung cancer, even his close friends were reluctant to give sincere compassion, instead waiting in hopes of being on the inside of a vintage and grotesque Andy Kaufman joke.

Further proof that overuses of the inside joke decimated his fan base was in the effort to resurrect Andy Kaufman on the big screen. Not even a superb performance by the great comic actor Jim Carey could fill the seats in this tribute film. Why?

Who wanted to make the film? ... Comic Actors.
Who helped sell the idea in Hollywood? ... Comic Actors.
Who did the movie? ... Comic Actors.
Who were the only people left on the inside of the inside joke? ...
Comic Actors.
Can you repeatedly fill movie houses with Comic Actors in the
audience?

They must have really enjoyed the diminishing quantities of humor
that Andy Kaufman dispensed in his waning days, and Andy must
have really needed the adoration of that last loyal fan base ... the
Comic Actors. The sharp, double-edged sword of the Theory of Finite
Humor cut both ways with Andy, even with his untimely death being
a joke. He and his cronies on the inside of the inside joke, both getting
what they deserved ... that the last laugh was on them!

~

This was one of the first stories I wrote just for the hell of it. This was a thought that lingered in my head long before I realized that I enjoyed writing. This was long before I realized it would be the lead off story in this classic tome years later. I am really glad that I put it on paper long ago, for no apparent reason. As the lead off it offers future writers, and practitioners of Apparent Logic some sound advice, and actually the first bit of advice that should be given. Chapter 16 is a tour through the curriculum at The Institute for the Theory & Practice of Apparent Logic where we will discuss the essential components of great Apparent Logic stories but …. Great Apparent Logic stories, along with great poems, novels, drawings, songs, essays, and toasts, may never reach another person's eyes and ears if the idea in its infancy is not captured in the first place.

Many times, I have encountered and engaged in a classic battle of opposing mental and physical forces, forces that can snuff out the tiny flame of creativity. This battle takes place as I am trying to fall asleep. Falling asleep for me has its stages. Lying flat on my back allows for all the weight of the day to slowly disappear. The prominent thoughts regarding events of the day and obligations of tomorrow take center stage as they get mentally checked off and leave consideration. Then I find myself on my side, eyes are tired, thoughts are quiet and I feel myself drifting off to sleep. That is when a creative thought emerges from the shadows of your brain! It may be remotely related to the day's events or not, but it finds its way to your consciousness because you have cleared the runway for it to land. Now the battle begins! Its existence now requires it to be dealt with. A task just when you don't want another task! For me, it activates a do-loop of sleep delaying thought.

"Hmmm, this creative nugget has some potential; let's think about it some more."
"OK, now it has taken a bit more shape"
"Is this thought worthy of capturing?"

24

"If I move, I will be that much further from sleep"
I know that capturing this thought means jotting it in notes on my phone, or sending it as a text to myself. Of course, I am on my side, facing away from my phone on my night table. I have to roll over to get it which cements that my near sleep will be destroyed, and a restart required.
"Can I just go to sleep and remember it tomorrow?"
This last question is the killer. I have previously answered to myself that I want this thought preserved. I can't risk losing it from memory.

You MUST capture it! From tiny acorns do great oaks grow! You must find the willpower to sacrifice the almost sleep for certainty of creative thought preservation. I promise, when you sit at your computer with your coffee the next morning, you will be so happy you have this little creative spark captured as your starting point for the next words to emerge from your keyboard. Take a look at one of my recent notes and chuckle. This thought was barely preserved in the dark as I punched letters haphazardly on my phone, but that thought made it into this book in the very late stage of its completion. You may recognize it at the end of the Yes, Wait … What? Segment.

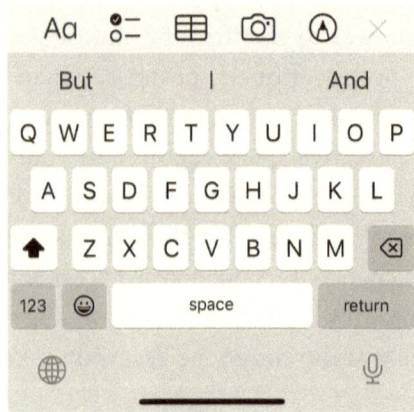

Ironically, you "feel" yourself drifting off by what you don't feel. If you have perused the table of contents, you will have seen that the subject of falling asleep rises to a level of significance to have its own chapter! In fact, I will give you a remedy for the restart of your sleep! So … Yes, I have given this writer's dilemma some considerable thought and feel this bit of advice is worthy of being in the front of this book.

CHAPTER IV

SHARING MARKET SHARES

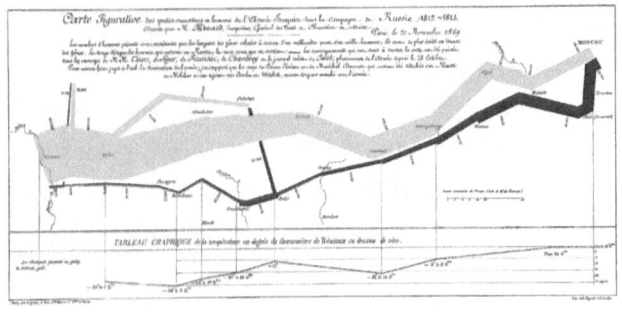

I t was an effort to settle conflicting data, which ultimately led to the formation of the idea generation process I call Catalytic Thinking, which is also the title of my first book. Look in the space between conflicting realities, and what you find may be very interesting.

Paradox: *"A statement that seems self-contradictory but in reality, expresses a possible truth."*
Oxymoron: *"A figure of speech that produces a self-contradictory effect."*

Paradox and his friend oxymoron like to hang out together. We all know an oxymoron when we see one, even if we forget what they are called. Jumbo shrimp is a classic oxymoron. Jumbo shrimp sounds logical, yet it doesn't make sense. Paradox is the more complicated of the two figures of speech, and while starting with a similar effect, it also exposes a grain of truth. Your first reaction grasps the incorrect nature of the expression, while your second reaction is the realization of the truth within. The old coach of the Yankees, Yogi Berra was famous for quotes that made you think twice. His description of a popular restaurant is a good paradox:

*"That place is so crowded that
nobody goes there anymore!"*

Paradox and oxymoron both provoke you, and people don't like to be provoked. If physically provoked, we fall back on our instinct of "fight-or-flight" and usually high tail it away from dangerous threats to life and limb. The other option is standing toe-to-toe and physically confronting provocations.

Paradox and oxymoron work in ways like physical provocation, in that they also make you fight or flee — just mentally, in this case. Using a "flight" scenario, you may have a response like, "That's the most idiotic thing I've heard of. I'm glad I don't have to give it another thought," or the logic-contorting statement you just heard could just be laughed off. In the "fight" mode, a provocation, i.e., a paradoxical statement, requires one to counteract the unsettling set of conflicting information with questions like "Why?" or "How can that be?" or "What's up with that?"

Let me give another example of the role of paradox and oxymoron, this time in workplace humor. I was in a regularly held meeting with people from sales and marketing, which was led by the General Manager. We all knew each other well, and we often dealt with matters in a humorous way but make no mistake, this general manager's meeting was also a serious, process-oriented work session. We were going through several slides, each listing market shares for our brands in about ten markets. Share numbers ranged from 10% to 30% for the given markets. The rallying cry was that we needed to drive each of these market shares up to at least 25%.

These slides were immediately followed by a series showing sales through six different distribution channels (Convenience Stores, Grocery, Food Service, etc.), with the percentage that each channel represented of the total, or the percent mix. Coincidentally, the percentages also ranged from 10% to 30% across *six* channels listed. As the discussion headed toward increasing a particular channel's percentage, I offered the rallying cry we had all just embraced: "We need to drive all these shares to at least 25%." Among the ten people in the room, there was an initial quick reaction to agree from several, including the general manager. At the same time, a couple of people did the necessary math, looked at my face and realized that I knew you cannot drive six shares to 25% when you are talking about a percentage of the total, it must equal 100%, so they began laughing as the power of the inside joke had taken effect.

Now bear this in mind: anyone in the General Manager's position would want their people to a) participate, and b) buy into what is being advocated, so his immediate reaction was one of welcoming this contribution, fully expecting that what I said was correct. He got caught in the apparent logic of a paradox until the evidence of laughter shattered his initial acceptance of my contribution. It had seemed all right, but it was wrong. Let me add that in a subsequent reorganization, coincidentally led by this General Manager, I was no longer in his regular meetings.

~

I have a special affection for this story for several reasons. This story was included in my first book called *Catalytic Thinking*, which was published a long time ago. It was the first use of the phrase "Apparent Logic!" Over the following years, the idea of apparent logic stuck with me and seemed to describe a verbal place that I liked to inhabit. I realized it was a thread in my stories and so in the recent years I have developed that concept to have its own special place in its own book, especially once inspired by Potter's *Gamesmanship*.

Another reason I love this story is that it happened in real life. It was an actual verbal interaction seized in the moment. I got to see all the faces in the room when the apparent logic bomb went off. My friend Jeff, who knows that something like that would come from me, well he caught it first and when we locked eyes, it took everything to not burst out laughing.

Then to see the GM's face go from happy I contributed to pissed-off that the joke was on him. That was priceless. And then to see the others gradually realize it was a joke, not because they got it, but only because they saw others laugh.

That conference room was my arena for the day, but you choose your own interaction to weave in a good dose of apparent logic where you see the chance. It doesn't need to be a long story, as in this case it was just one line, brilliantly dropped.

Oh, and bonus points if you know the significance of the chart at the start of this chapter. Well done! It is Charles Joseph Menard's chart of Napoleon's ill-fated march on Moscow in 1812. While it plots seven different variables, you need only look at the thickness of the tan bar and the black bar. That shows the number of troops Napoleon started with and ended with ... a horribly costly gambit. Russia wins wars with climate and geography.

Look up Edward R. Tufte, an artist and brilliant mathematician who has been called the "Leonardo da Vinci" of data. In his acclaimed book called The Visual Display of Quantitative Information, Tufte labels Minard's chart as "Probably the best statistical chart ever drawn." The highest praise from the leading savant on the subject.

Funny, but it was Jeff who gave me Tufte's book. He should be glad I'm putting his kind gesture to good use.

CHAPTER V

WRITTEN, SPOKEN, HEARD

This story is purely a product of circumstance. It is the natural product of unplanned events being in a great sequence. There was nothing tying these events together, nor was there any reason for them to be so. Until the picture. We were on a golf trip in Scotland. My first time there, so I had nothing to do with the itinerary, as far as the golf schedule was concerned. But there was one site I wanted to see, if possible, and it was possible right after we landed in Edinburgh. Not far away was Rosslyn Chapel! Made famous in The DaVinci Code, it was the beautiful, ornate, little chapel that was said to have kept the secrets of the Jesus and Mary bloodline, as well as the Templar treasures spirited out of France when the King purged the Templars in 1309. In addition to this history, the Rosslyn Chapel is one of the most ornate religious structures ever built. Every inch has carvings, and the eight columns inside were each carved by different artists with different designs. If I recall correctly, one young apprentice carved a column so ornate that he embarrassed his superiors and was executed for his boldness. Suffice it to say, it is well worth a stop on any kind of trip to the area. It is stunning.

So, we did, and we snapped a bunch of pictures, one of which stood out.

Red-eyed from the red eye flight there, but so happy to be on Scottish land, we were filled with surprise at this very cool place ... those were the ingredients for this peculiar picture. To anyone it should scream: "1970s English Rock Band Album Cover!" Ok, maybe not Led Zeppelin level, but surely Renaissance Live at Rosslyn Chapel!

So, to me, this picture needed another life. It needed to be shared. My only outlet then was Facebook, which I was not a very active participant. I scan through my account and see that some time earlier I had posted this picture:

Well, the Nashville trip was to see a Hall of Fame musician later in his career, Burt Bacharach! It was an amazing experience; one I will never forget. Wow, just as this book is a tribute to the book I got from my dad, this story is a tribute to the music I got from my folks. Burt Bacharach and Herb Alpert!

So now we have two unrelated pictures, and a story to be told. Now there is a choice. I want you all to realize that moments of inflection are just waiting to happen. To most, there are only two paths. The Truth and a Lie. I didn't want either. The truth is sometimes tiresome. It is conveyed in words that have been used over and over. I could say three words about Rosslyn Chapel and a listener, more knowledgeable than me could finish the sentence. When I am telling the story, I don't want to be interrupted by some know-it-all, so the best way to avoid that is to lead the story in places that no other person could ever anticipate.

The catalyst just happened to present itself, and I posted this on Facebook with the picture of us at Rosslyn Chapel:

==============================

Well, now that my meetings in Nashville have borne fruit, I can now divulge to you the results of a few years late-night efforts.

You see, my primary reason to visit Nashville recently was to meet with record producers. And the picture above will be the artwork on the cover of my first album!

This album is entitled *"**Written, Spoken, Heard** ... One man's tribute to well-chosen words"* and it contains a compilation of up-tempo Gregorian chants ... but get this! Mine are translated into English!

Early feedback has been decidedly negative, such as *"disturbing, while at the same time disorienting,"* and the claim that *"what is on the album is neither up-tempo, nor remotely Gregorian, nor even chants,"* so I've got that going for me.

In fact, my first producer (no longer in my employ) showed his total lack of knowledge about where entertainment is heading when he stormed out of a creative session where I introduced the album title ... screaming, *"You call this a tribute to well-chosen words but it is nothing but fucking vowels strung together and sounded out!"*

I normally do not use profanity in my writing but to honor the last words that he chose, I chose to leave that in.

That silly man should have heeded the old proverb, *"Better to remain silent and have them think you a fool, than post shit on Facebook and prove it to them."* Anyway, I digress.

So, while the content has not yet garnered critical acclaim, I feel the cover-art alone will propel this venture forward. Do you agree? And does anyone recognize the significant religious architecture in the picture? Chant on!

～

The response was amazingly supportive
of my new musical career!
But what many failed to realize,
is that Facebook post was on 4/1/16

April Fool's Day!

The scaffolding of truth was the pictures.
Quoting the record producer added credibility.
This post was almost 10 years ago.

Guess who played at the Wall Street Theater
in Norwalk, CT recently?

A Gregorian Chant band!

CHAPTER VI

THE GREATEST GRAFFITI EVER

I drive quite a bit all over the Northeast. With all that time, I take notice of my surroundings as I travel. For example, I like to judge roadside billboards to see if I think they are on target or missing their mark with their intended message. While many are way off target, in my opinion, there is a bigger pet peeve about billboards. When are those marketing geniuses going to understand that if I can't read it all in the couple of seconds that I am given, then it shouldn't contain that much message? And if you're going to purposely break that common courtesy of communication, then I don't trust you.

Well, anyway, one day I was driving up Route 8 in Connecticut to go to a golf course. Route 8 is a sort of connector highway through the countryside east of Danbury. It's a 55 mile per hour stretch of road laid out to get you to the next town. In some places, it is carved out of the mountainside, exposing sheer rock faces on each side. These are prime places for local teens to identify themselves with some type of graffiti. You've seen it before, usually in the form of an allegiance to the local high school team. "Raiders Rule" or "Warriors Forever" or something like that. Occasionally you'll see such avant-garde graffiti as "Wendy Loves Randy" or "Tigers Suck." It must be a right similar to an animalistic ritual of marking a territory. So, there I was cruising down this stretch of road trying to make a tee time, and there on a huge, prominent rock wall were these words:

"OUR NAMES"

I glanced at this, and didn't give it another thought until quite some time down the road when it hit me. I was well past the place where the graffiti was emblazoned on the rock, close to never thinking about it again, but something kept me hanging on to this strange epitaph. Then, in one moment of clairvoyance, it became crystal clear. I saw the exact scenario that led to the creation of that big, painted rock that screamed out to all motorists; "OUR NAMES." I laughed for a very long time.

. . .

The basement of Brian's parent's house was one of those converted to accommodate kids and their friends. Brian's parents had four kids and enjoyed the times when the neighborhood friends came over to their house to hang out, because that meant that Brian's parents did not have to drive Brian somewhere else or pick him up. Brian's parents were social people and liked hosting events as much as going to them. Brian didn't mind. His folks were pretty cool, and his friends liked the accommodations at Brian's house, especially when Brian's parents were away.

Brian was on the high school football team, as an underweight defensive halfback. He did pretty well tackling guys who ran by him, without getting himself hurt too bad. He loved the camaraderie of the team. The "Demons" were an OK team, and this is where he was befriended by Greg, the bigger, more athletic, more popular, but still somewhat insecure quarterback of the team. Since they lived near each other, they hung out in a sort of symbiotic relationship. Brian loved the company of Greg and all the popularity that came with it. Greg loved hanging out with Brian because Brian was their mouth-piece. Brian knew just what to say, whether to girls, parents, or amongst the guys. What came from Brian's mouth was always some-thing that Greg could take and add to, or act upon. Paul was friends with Brian, not through athletics, but because they shared a devotion to off-beat music, bands that screamed lyrics that espoused the virtues of being an outsider. They also liked to fish together, which is why Greg could put up with, and even like, Paul in a tolerant sort of way. These were good kids, not out to get into major trouble, but certainly, in their hormonal prime, not immune to the powers of peer pressure, especially combined with the deadliest of teenage curses: the need to show off in front of the opposite sex.

That night in late July, Brian's folks were away, and Brian was hanging out with Paul and Greg in the basement, shooting pool and cranking tunes. Of course, they called Angela. Brian put Greg up to it and, sure enough, he called her. Angela was one of the pretty cheer-leaders at the high school. Pretty and outgoing and daring and just confident enough to accept their invite to come over and "hang out".

Angela was no dope, and picked up her friend Cindy, who she was going to the movies that night with, anyway. Cindy was also on the cheerleader squad, as there was not a huge turnout for the cheerleader tryouts that year. Cindy was full of enthusiasm, team spirit and loyalty. She could best be described in a complementary but true line from a Bruce Springsteen song. "You ain't a beauty, but hey, you're all right." Since the alibi was set for the two of them, they had time to kill and why not go over to Brian's house? They were cranking tunes, talking about the Demons, and they had some beer that Brian's folks left unattended. Wow! Besides, Angela could like Greg if he only could show some sort of interest in her. To help her own cause, she also convinced Cindy that Paul had expressed an interest in her! Hey, even though Paul wasn't on the football team, he wasn't a jerk. He was still a decent looking acne-faced kid who was just going in a different direction.

But what about Brian's intentions? Well, heck, why wouldn't he think that Angela might, one day in his dreams, shed her going-no-where hope that Greg takes his mind off football long enough to see that she exists and see Brian as the answer to her romantic dreams? Hey, it might be a long shot, but that's what high school is all about, hoping for that long shot to come in. Brian knew that Greg was the "raison d'etre" for Angela, but he liked the chance to spend more time in her company, on his long-term project of ever subtly trying to divert her affections toward him. By the way, it wouldn't be a long-term project if Brian didn't have some success with this endeavor. Don't ever forget the win over the Garnets last year, where Brian made out with Angela at the post-game bonfire in what became an unspeakable, never told, mutually understood, momentary flash of brilliance, that Brian always cherished, Angela never felt guilty about, and actually, always wondered about.

Maybe I should say at this point that the names have been changed from my high school experience so as not to confuse anyone who actually knows me. But really, the story is about Brian, Greg, Paul, Angela and Cindy, on that hot July night.

In that moment on Route 8, some three miles past the "OUR

NAMES" graffiti, I had a vision of these kids in the basement, slightly drunk, acting out their different roles:

Angela: *"Greg, how are we going to beat the Garnets this year?"*
Brian: *"Greg's got a plan that is sure to win this year, right Greg?"*
Greg: *"Yeah, we're gonna kick their asses!"*
Paul: *"Cindy do you like the Violent Femmes?"*
Cindy: *"Yeah, turn it up."*
Brian: *"We need to let the Garnets know that we're gonna kick their asses; how are we gonna do that Angela?"*
Angela: *"What do you want me to do my cheer on main street in their town?"*
Brian: *"I'd like to see that."*
Angela: (quietly, to Brian (so cruel)) *"Only if you're the only one there."*
Brian: *"Say when."*
Greg (oblivious to Brian and Angela's sidebar flirting): *"Why don't we spray paint on the big rock on Route 8, 'Garnets Suck'!"*

A big laugh is let out by everyone, in part due to the actual finite quantity of humor in what Greg said, and in part because, after all, a group laughter kind of neutralizes all the weird tension in the room.

Brian: (bringing logic back to the train of thought) *"We can't do that because they'll know it's us. Greg, they'll come right to you."*

A quiet moment envelops the room. The song Blister in the Sun is on, so it's not uncomfortable for no one to be speaking. Everyone is sizing up their chances, solidifying their presumed positions vis-a-vis one another with eye contact, and thinking of what to say next, without hurrying. That was long enough for Brian to come up with his idea.

Brian: *"Forget saying we're gonna kick their asses. Let's put our names on the big rock!!"*
Greg & Cindy: (Almost automatically, since that's the way they worked) *"Yeah ... let's do it!"*

Don't forget the two unstoppable powers at work here: Peer Pressure and the desire to impress the opposite sex.

Paul: *"We can't paint our names on the f---in rock! How stupid is that?! Why don't we just go to the Police station and turn ourselves in?"*

Important part here. I don't know if Brian meant it when he said it, or if he was quick enough to turn lemons into lemonade. I think it was in an inspiration created by Angela looking at Brian with a look that was reminiscent of the bon-fire night, when Brian looked at his ever present, reliable go-to guy Greg and said:

Brian: *"We're not going to put our names up there; we're going to put "OUR NAMES" up there!!!"*

Now, of course, only Greg and Brian knew that they were only going to spray the letters that form the two words "O-U-R N-A-M-E-S" on that big old rock. The fact that Paul, Angela and Cindy thought they were going to spray paint their actual names, and maybe even their god-damned phone numbers on the rock, only scared them even more.

Remember the **"Theory of Finite Humor"**? Remember how the finite amount of humor gets divided up among only those who get it? How cool did Brian and Greg feel? How psyched were they that they had an inside joke that was scaring the hell out of Paul, Angela, and Cindy?

Each, for their own reasons wanted to carry this out to impress their own intended party—Brian to impress Greg, Brian to impress Angela, Greg because he was going to spray paint "Garnets Suck" no matter what he had to do to get everyone there, and also to keep the joke going because Brian wanted to. Cindy because she wanted to do what Angela thought was okay to do, Paul because he didn't care what trouble he got into, and the girls were leading him there. Brian because he realized that his idea was one they could actually carry out, without getting into trouble, and that it would get them out of his house and maybe give a chance for him to be alone with Angela while Greg was spray painting—all worthy causes! And so it was, on that July night.

I saw this Greatest Graffiti ever, many years ago, and assume that it had been there for a couple of years prior to that, much to the delight of Brian, Greg, Paul, Angela and Cindy. That remarkable evening, probably in 1993, they all got what they hoped for. And to our delight, they left us with a great example of "Out-of-the-box-thinking" to view as we drive by.

There is tremendous irony in this story. The brilliance in their graffiti is in its blatant prominence, while maintaining complete anonymity. Instead of writing their actual names, they wrote "OUR NAMES" and only those who were there that night, and those they told, know the truth about who did it. Even those they told cannot turn them in. Can you see the cops questioning them? It would be like a bad take-off on Abbott & Costello's " Who's on First"

Cops: *"Alright Brian, did you write our names on the big rock?"*
Brian: *"Seeing how I only just met you, I couldn't have written your names up there."*
Cops: *"You know what I mean; did you write your names up there?"*
Brian: *"It doesn't say your names, it says our names."*
Cops: *"Ok ... our names, did you do it?"*
Brian: *"No, we didn't write our names on the rock; you wouldn't have to ask me if we did, would you?"*
Cops: *"But it says our names up there."*
Brian: *"Why'd you write your names up there? You're in trouble, ya know."*

While brilliantly anonymous, after one glance on the road that day, I knew exactly who did it. I only ask that the real Brian, Greg, Paul, Angela and Cindy email me to tell how the actual events of that night differed from my version. Whatever the case, I got a great laugh out of it.

Well, I already confessed in the previous paragraph to making up this story so the suspense about whether it is real versus made up is voided. I can tell you that when I shared it with close friends to read, I did get one person to ask, *"Did this really happen that way?"*

An important take away from that question is that it could have! The detailed account given is as real as the real story; however that story unfolded. The concept of "voluminous detail" comes to mind as will be explained more thoroughly in the last chapter about the curriculum of the Institute for the Theory & Practice of Apparent Logic. When imagining the group of kids and the dynamics that guided them, the picture in my head became that clear. Way past generalizations, such that the details became vivid if you just let your mind see them. Ask yourself questions as you are viewing the current scenario in your head and those answers will fill out the "Nth" level details.

Each next level of details adds to the credibility built from the previous level. This is especially helpful in the case, such as this story, where you are starting with ZERO factual information. The only input for the story were the two words: *"Our Names."* We are building credibility out of thin air, a pretty cool trick, if I may say so myself.

In the old days, wizards practiced alchemy trying to turn lead into gold. Apparent Logic turns flimsy stories into compelling stories.

CHAPTER VII

SAVING OUR NATIONAL PASTIME

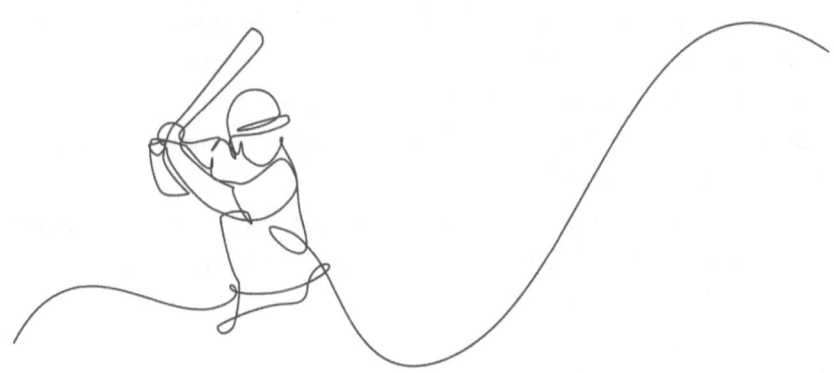

OK friends, I am going to share with you one of the beautiful things about self-publishing, which is how my previous book, *Catalytic Thinking*, and this book were brought to life. With the traditional route of a big book publishing company, you have a pesky editor who will impose strict literary rules upon the Author. Rules like every chapter of the book should support what the title of the book is trying to convey. But! When you self-publish the book, you can take liberties with the rules in hopes that as you risk breaking the flow somewhat, you hope the reader enjoys what you offer with a new but not perfectly related chapter.

That's where we are here.

While not filled with Apparent Logic content, this chapter is the result of one of the key dynamics that will free your mind to allow Apparent Logic to visit your thoughts. That dynamic is the power of observation and questioning. DaVinci's lament was that people look but don't see. I agree. To prove DaVinci's point, I am going to make an observation that few, if any people, see even though it is right before their eyes around 180 times per year.

The sad thing is, I made this observation back in the year 2000, and in the last 20-plus years that observation is still true, and the question "Why?" is still applicable.

What sport has laid claim to this lofty description: "Our National Pastime?"
That's right ... Baseball.

Now, what is the only professional sport where the players do not shake hands at the end of a game, or especially a playoff series?
That's right again ... Baseball.

Please ponder and enjoy this letter that I wrote and sent to Bobby Valentine of the NY Mets, and Joe Torre of the NY Yankees, when they met in the *"Subway Series,"* World Series in 2000.

Mets & Yankees Organization
October 16th, 2000
Dear Joe and Bobby,

Please consider this. It's past midnight and I am writing this after watching the Yanks join the Mets in what will be the greatest series of our time. I **urge** you to **not** be just content with that fact. I have an idea that will put the most positive stamp on the game and will cement your place in defining what this series will mean to everyone, fans and casual spectators alike.

My name is Pete Steer, and my idea has the potential to transcend sports and impact life in a bigger way. You can make this impact. What's missing from baseball is **The Gesture.** The gesture that is sorely lacking from our Nation's pastime … is to line up and shake hands with the opponents after the game, win or lose.

.

I think it is pathetic that a baseball team immediately celebrates their good fortune; while their worthy opponents and coaches are dismissed to the dugout. *All* other sports show more sportsmanship than that. Every Little Leaguer knows that at the end of the game, you line up at home base and shake hands! But the Boys of Summer don't??? Those competitors on the losing side deserve better, and especially when those individuals are New York's own! I am damn proud of each player on each New York team for what they did to get us into this Subway Series; as I know each of you are too. Don't let the losing side be belittled, ignored, and go unappreciated while the winners celebrate in such a self-centered manner. As they say "Act like you've been there before," which for the Mets has been twice and for the Yankees 27 times!

We all know it has been since 1956 since this chance last visited our city. Put your mark on it this time around in a way that lasts well beyond the next chance. Line up man-to-man to shake hands and say *"Great game...great series"* to every last competitor. Do it in front of the fans before heading off into your role as celebratory victors and worthy opponents. The media want to make this out to be a gang fight. Instead, both of your organizations have a heritage of class that warrants this "Gesture." It would be a great gift to our National Pastime from our citizens of New York.

By the way, I will Fed-Ex this to each of you every day until the series last game. Thanks very much for your consideration.

Pete Steer

This letter was included in my previous book as an example of Malcom Gladwell's assertion in *The Tipping Point*, that little actions can have a big impact. Now keep in mind these things and you'll understand my motives a little better:

I am not even a very good baseball fan by any standard. I get caught up in the game usually in the playoffs only.

What effort did it take to create this "Little Action"? Not much. A half hour to write the letter. A couple of bucks to send it. Oh … and withstanding the incredible grief my friends heaped on when I showed them this letter as we went to the 2nd game of the series. That was the major hurdle. They thought I was crazy, but they also did not know my end game in sending this letter, which follows.

It was not crazy to think that this letter might have elicited a response from either Joe Torre's organization or Bobby Valentine's organization. It was not crazy to think that Joe could have called Bobby, or vice versa, to say:

"Hey, did you get that letter about The Gesture?"
"Yeah … I was gonna call you. What do you think?"
"Well, the guy is a nut case, but it's a great idea."
"Yeah … lets do it!"

From there, they actually line up and shake hands after the last game, creating a positive stir not seen in a sporting event in a long time. Bob Costas goes wild about "The Gesture" adding great historical sporting context to the event, pontificating about the greater need for sportsmanship and civility in our everyday lives. Sportswriters and other media folks add their two cents, amplifying the Gesture. Joe and Bobby are hailed for their judgement to make "The Gesture" a reality, both give credit for the idea where it belongs. The letter is circulated throughout the press.

I use the ensuing media attention to demand greater positive social change take place … and, oh yeah, to promote my book.

From there, who knows what could have happened?

So, I include this chapter because there is still work to do. No, they did not shake hands in that Subway Series. Although this letter was written twenty-four years ago, the need today is even greater. It is June 2024, and I just watched the Met's win a great series against the Phillies … in London! We brought our "National Pastime" to the Brits to expand the audience base for baseball. Well, guess what? The British fans are used to watching soccer—where at the end of the game the opposing players put arms around each other and trade jerseys. What did our two teams do after the last exciting game? One celebrated victory amongst their own team members, while the other team skulked off to the locker room, not one hand shaken. Terribly disappointing and even worse is that nobody is pointing it out.

Next October, two teams will contest the World Series once again. Maybe you can connect with someone from those teams and implore them to bring "The Gesture" to life! A handshake at home plate and a *"G'Game!"* are sorely missing.

It's not like making the best-seller list, and it's not like seeing your cartoon in the New Yorker, and it's not like creating a word or phrase that enters our lexicon, but …

I wouldn't mind if, in my part-time avocation of writing about something that took a half hour of effort, I wouldn't mind that the result was saving our National Pastime.

CHAPTER VIII

ILLUMINATION! OH GREAT MYSTERY REVEALED!

By the title of my first book, *"Catalytic Thinking, How Wild Bird Seed Inspired a Mid-life Epiphany,"* I may have given you the impression that there was some great mystery resolved that led to the creation of my ideation process. "From wild bird seed comes a mid-life epiphany" sort of conjures up the image of some divine intervention, as if lighting struck me, leaving me a different, more clairvoyant person. For those of you hoping, and perhaps needing to hear a scenario like this, well, here it is.

It was an eerie late autumn afternoon on the barrier beach near a confluence of conflicted water called "The Gut," the farthest point by over-sand vehicle on the eastern tip of Martha's Vineyard. Eerie in that one panoramic view of the horizon showed both of our most influential heavenly bodies. A look towards the island revealed the still-warm, fiery orb that, combined with temperature changes, percolates the instinctual clock in every single living thing in the area by screaming "your time is running out this year, get what you need and get going!" A look toward the water, toward Cape Cod, startled your eyes and logic with the sight of another celestial body, almost as large and nearly the same color, just hovering above the water. This one could be called "The Great Emphasizer," as its influence every 28 days, bolds and underscores the sun's message by pulling the water to its greatest heights, covering with water parts of the beach not reached since the previous winter's storms. This prolonged and deepened high tide allows game fish both the extra time, and the depth of water, to charge into the shallows to fill up on the trapped schools of baitfish. "The Great Emphasizer," the late Autumn full moon, creates a most abundant buffet spread for the stripers and bluefish that I was seeking with my 9-weight fly rod, inciting a frenzied, reckless feeding pattern.

It never fails to give me the greatest sense of urgency I have ever felt, and I can imagine it to be a feeling parallel to that running through the marauding stripers. As if that isn't enough, "The Great Emphasizer" pulls double duty a long six hours later, and almost with a bit of sarcasm it strips the water on the ebb tide to such low depths it lays bare the bottom of the ocean. You'd swear that lakes must be overflowing somewhere else in the world, as you imagine the moon saying "that was just in case you thought me and the sun were kidding, go on, get out of here!" It gives you the feeling that you've forgotten something not just that day, but in your lifetime. Everything is a celebration of the present moment because it will all be gone in one quick change of the wind. Everything is hurried and fills you with the hopes that you are truly prepared. Now, there is no second chance.

I stood watching what I believed to be the last school of stripers, just out of reach of my cast and heading further away. Another season ending—the incredible emptiness is palpable. Another cycle is almost completed. Unaware of my own actions, I found myself on the roof of my '77 Toyota Land Cruiser, you know, the one with a map of the Vineyard beaches shellacked to the interior roof and covered with pictures of past fishing seasons, right, the blue one. Fly rod draped down onto the hood like a military presentation of arms, I was sitting cross-legged with two fist-fulls of birdseed pulled from a huge bag in the back of the Land Cruiser. Why? Probably because my hands needed to act out physically, what my mind could only urge, *grasp something amidst everything fleeting*. I held arms outstretched, one fist just above and windward of each heavenly body, letting the birdseed sift through my fingers so it combined with wind and gravity to cross each the sun and moon, providing what seemed like to me a filter. Looking at the seed pass before the sun's waning orange glow, then turning to see the seeds passing through the moon's cold yellow back-drop. This filtering lens seemed to be able to decipher the dual message in the singular act of autumn turning to winter. A season ends, causing as much reflection about the "all" as it does about the moment, the totality as if it were being handed in as is.

Your mind is yelling at you, *"Did I bring ... ?" "Do I have ... ?" "Will I see ... ?" "Did I lock the ...?" "Did I turn off the ... ?"* If you have read Sebastian Junger's chilling account, in *The Perfect Storm*, of your brain's effort to function as oxygen is deprived while drowning, you'd know that the thoughts that run through your mind in the near final moments are as inane as those above. They are not the soul-searching ones you'd expect. This only added to the sense of eeriness. There on the beach, my mind seemed to be working in the same pattern, but with more time and more oxygen. The closing of a season, the completing of a cycle, has your brain shifting metaphors to also ask: "What if I had ... ?" "Did I say good bye to ... ?" "Was I a good ... ?"

In that moment, when stillness and timelessness offered the most crystal-clear view of cathartic, chaotic, hurried change ... that's when it hit me.

I am told that I bellowed:

"Illumination! Oh great mystery revealed!!!"

Just before falling backwards off the Land Cruiser onto a big rock.

What I do remember upon waking the next day at the Martha's Vineyard Hospital with bandages on my head, was first a feeling of dizziness, then that strange feeling that I was supposed to remember something. After life was pumped back into me, by virtue of coffee brought fresh from the Dock Street Coffee Shop, my buddies enjoyed making sport of my plight. I wasn't laughing as much as they were, not because of the pounding in my head, but because of that strange feeling.

What was I supposed to remember???

After they left, and when I could again focus on something for more than 10 seconds, I noticed some paper next to my bed with drawings and my very illegible handwriting.

There was, of my own hand, this diagram ...
and the explanation for how ideas are formed.

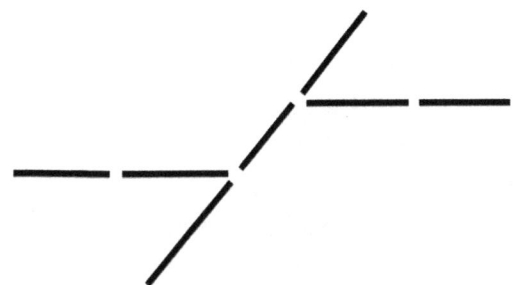

Pretty cool, huh? In a way, I wish it were like that. As a fisherman, I know the beauty of a really good story. One that has enough wild facts in it so it can more easily disguise the exaggerations and outright fabrications that must inevitably find their way in.

But I am, and you are, fortunate that the story didn't happen that way. I'm fortunate because I would have missed all of the self-awareness capabilities that I now have from the years of pondering the Creative Process, and my involvement with it. You are fortunate because what I have laid out for you in *Catalytic Thinking* is a lot more actionable, and a lot less painful, than a good whack on the noggin.

By the way ... that diagram inspired me to write my book *Catalytic Thinking*. It is a visual depiction of a quote by Dorothy Leonard, once a Professor of Innovation at Harvard. She said:

"Breakthrough creativity occurs at the intersection of two previously unconnected trains of thought."

That diagram shows those trains of thought connecting, sharing concepts, and moving in new, breakthrough directions.

Catalytic Thinking

Creating Positive Change and
Breakthrough Ideas!
or...
How Wild Bird Seed
Inspired a Mid-life Epiphany!

by Pete Steer

CHAPTER IX

WANT TO GET TO SLEEP FASTER? STOP TOUCHING YOURSELF!

Ok ... we all want the first part and are all guilty of the second part. But there is a big misunderstanding! I don't mean touching yourself like that! No! This has to do with shutting off your body's messaging system, not activating it. Everyone thinks that just by jumping under the covers, you will be ready for deep sleep.

But we make a mistake in the preparation, or lack thereof. Under the covers, our legs touch each other, our knees do, our hands fold on our chest. All of that sends an overload of information to your brain, or at least twice as much as it needs. One part of your body is sending info to the brain, and another is duplicating that message. That is called *"Impulse Redundancy."* You won't get to sleep fast in a state of Impulse Redundancy as your brain is as active as an O'Hare traffic controller on a holiday weekend.

It is the difference between "Touch" and "Feel." One knee touches the other, while the other knee feels that same interaction. Two messages to the brain, twice as much shit to process before you can sleep. That's what synapses are; they are the spark plug that fires off when activated. So, don't activate them. Keep your body down to one message only to the brain, so it is easier to shut off.

Do this by having a pillow, or part of the duvet cover between every part of your body.

Nothing touches anything. No knees against knees, no ankles crossing ankles, nor hands against hands ... in order to fall asleep quicker. Since your body already knows the feel of the pillow, which will not positively act against your body ... it will calm itself. Twice as fast. This state is called *"Impulse Singularity,"* and it is the gateway where the fastest path to sleep exists. Ditch all the other sleep aids and go natural.

Here is a way to see this in action. We all take naps on the couch. In those cases, tiredness and sleepy eyes give you all you need to get to sleep, even with legs crossed and arms across your chest. But have you ever either woken like that, or have been conscious just before falling asleep? When you find yourself in that state, pause ... don't move a muscle. Keeping your eyes closed, try to determine if your feet are crossed. Since you were so close to sleep, you are experiencing all messages shut off, and you will probably not know which foot is crossed over the top of the other, or even if they are crossed at all! This is the desired state that allows sleep and it is called *"Impulse Hibernation."* As soon as you move your feet and find they are indeed crossed, you will get messages from both feet and your brain will be far from being able to sleep again. Or at least twice as far. Your brain can shut off one message from a foot noticing the covers far quicker that it can shut down two feet feeding simultaneous messages to the brain that one of them had a sense of Feel and the other had a sense of Touch, and then for each of them to send the opposite message that they had Touch when they had Feel and the other had Feel when they also had Touch! Get it?

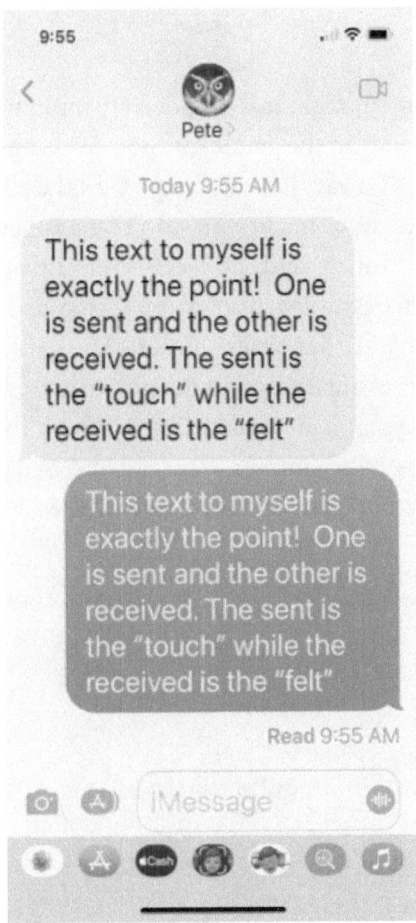

Separate all body parts with luxurious covers and pillows and I am sure you will see a faster path to deep sleep. And for those of you who thought in order to get to sleep faster you shouldn't touch yourself the other way ... well I may need to study that too ... and will need some volunteers. ;-)

~

This story came about from just wondering, upon waking from a nap, are my legs crossed at the ankle or not. Waking without moving, which would give it away. Just wake up and take account of yourself. You'd be surprised how much you don't know because it had been shut off. Both the "Touch" and the "Feel." Out of that obscure observation, I realized that is the state of sleep. Sleep achieved after all the tossing and turning. All synopses shut off. So … if that's what it looks like, it made me wonder how you get there from being awake standing next to your bed hoping like hell you can fall asleep fast. What gets in the way of jumping into bed and being in dreamy land? It is the time it takes to shut down nerve impulses. Follow this path…

"Impulse Redundancy"
to
"Impulse Singularity"
to
"Impulse Hibernation"

CHAPTER X

BEMORPHOUS SOCCER

Ok, who doesn't love high school soccer? When you are in it—you are in it. So, I got in it, deep, and had the most rewarding experience. I'd like you to hear a great story. My son, Nick, went through all the youth soccer teams and made his best friends along the way. That whole trajectory points toward the varsity team in the senior year of high school. By that time, friends are fast and well known. At that age, together, they feel like they can conquer great heights.

But the magic only really happens when there is one great year of offspring. That happened in 1996. All of us were having our first children, and it created a great soccer team by senior year at Ridgefield High School.

So, the kids of that year gelled as they went from swarm ball—where little kids just run to the ball and start kicking. Then on to developing their skills ... each finding their own spot on the field based on their skills. Some quick and with foot skills went up top as strikers. That was Killian, Bonnie, and Dan. Some with good presence on the field and knowing how to transition from defense to offense became mid-fielders. That was Dean, Adam, and Tom, who could dribble in a way to keep the ball close to their feet, away from the opponent's feet. Others with a bigger presence became defenders. That's where Meegs, Cass, and Tyler fortified the back line. Meegs controlled the back field with attitude. And not the attitude you would think. It wasn't so much with meanness, rather he played with joy. Joy of competition. Joy of just being part of this team, and joy in thwarting the opponent's efforts. And then there was the last line of defense, Nick as goalkeeper, a great stopper of shots while amassing quite a collection of bruises and concussions along the way.

Coach Bergen was at the helm, with his storied history as a player for the same team. Coach Bergen played for Ridgefield long ago and helped the team win its first two state championships against the perennial favorite Glastonbury. Then, coach got the third state title against the same Glastonbury in the year a few ahead of Nick's grade. Three titles accomplished by the time Nick's team became seniors.

. . .

The Logo

That year, I volunteered to lead the soccer Booster Club, doing fundraising and helping with this year's merchandise. Nick had been drawing up some designs for our warmup jackets, which just had a tiger face on them. Here is the existing logo at the time. A little too much tiger, a little too much detail, and it doesn't scream out Soccer.

Nick created a logo much more closely resembling the great crests of the English Premier League, and it looked great. He got the team, the Coach, and the Athletic Director to approve it and the team sported this new logo.

The orange and black for the school colors and three stars signifying the three state Championships in the school's history. I'd like to think the new logo and new look may have played a little part in their success that year. Ok, more about the team.

The Improbable Situation

The team finished regular season making both the regional and state tournaments. After a tough loss to a mighty Greenwich team in the regional tourney, the team was preparing for the states. That's when I got the call from the Coach. He had arranged for the team to play a "friendly" against a college team that had former players that he had coached at the high school. That game was 3 days away. All good, but then he added, *"Due to a family emergency, I will be out of town ... would you coach the team?"*

I yelled *"Yes! Wait ... what?"* I couldn't take back the Yes, nor did I want to, but holy smokes, really? I've never coached at this level. But ... with my two boys we have analyzed the sport of soccer in depth as we follow Everton in the EPL and of course when players are representing their nations in the World Cup. I enjoy the occasional impreciseness of soccer, like how you take a throw-in from the general area where the ball went out. You get about five yards of leeway to keep the game flowing. Then on the other hand an offsides call can be reviewed by the virtual assistant referee (VAR) down to the players eyelash!

Suffice it to say, I have opinions on how the game could (or should) be played. Not just opinions but ideas that have been tested verbally amongst us. And now...I have just been given the perfect petri dish to try them out. This game is with skilled players, and the outcome doesn't really matter. It is not a school sanctioned game and doesn't count towards anything. The expectation is that our high school players will lose but gain wisdom from playing with better players. There is no downside, and the upside might as well be invisible, since no one is even looking for it. I told Coach Bergen the team is in good hands.

At practice the next day the Coach had me attend and told the team he had to leave. "Coach Steer will cover practice today and tomorrow and for the game." The kids showed the feeling you get when a substitute teacher shows up: like we don't have to do anything! And they also showed some curiosity about what the next three days will be like. Coach Bergen leaves and it gets quiet. Expecting me to start practice by sending them for five laps around the field, they relaxed when I just started talking and not coaching. They were taking a knee, or sitting, all in a group.

I was walking around the team as I spoke. I told them what this one game opportunity holds for them. It is a one-off chance to learn. No big expectations on outcome, meaning a loss to this college team was the likely outcome. Good prep for high-level play expected in the state tourney. I delivered all that and then said nothing as the team, each person at a time, absorbed the low, but realistic expectation.

Changing the Game

Then I said, *"You know ... it doesn't have to be that way."* Attentions now focused. *"Do you want to play the most fun soccer game you've played AND take a victory away from a college team?"*

Cheers from the players as they adjusted their focus as if they were now watching a high-wire act waiting for the man to fall.

We gathered around and talked. I directed the conversation around two main questions: What are our chances of winning? And how do we improve the chances? We all agreed quickly on the answer to the first question—the odds are very low. Our team is mostly seniors in high school, while their squad would be mostly juniors and seniors in college. It was good that we all agreed on this simple level-setting start because I wanted to build a succession of agreements

69

from the team, knowing how important agreement will be in later strategy.

Any conversation about who will win a soccer match will include who scores the first goal. We know soccer is a low-scoring game (please, no comments about the game being boring because it is low scoring). So, the first goal is almost essential. If scored by the team favored, it establishes dominance and a sense of an inevitable, pre-determined outcome. If scored by the underdog, well, that carries a lot of weight in that it flusters the favored opponent. The reason is the favored team cannot fall into auto-mode, and the underdog team with the first goal sends a resounding disruptive shock into the match, which is borne out by the stunning statistic that the team with the first goal wins 70 percent of the time. It doesn't say which team. Just be the team that scores first. That is the brass ring. And to boot (pun intended) your chances of not losing the game when you score first skyrocket to 88 percent.

The 30-Minute Game and the 60-Minute Game

So, our team bought into scoring first as the primary tactic to "improve our chances." Next, I introduced another stat that is readily available, and that is the average time it takes in a game for the first goal to be scored. That is thirty minutes into a game. I had looked these two stats up because I had been thinking about an approach that could capitalize on this information. So now I have the team on board that we need to get the first goal and we only have thirty minutes to do it. Perfect. We need a strategy to play a thirty-minute game with less than conventional methods to come out on top 1-0 after thirty minutes and then we have a sixty-minute game in which we have a 70 percent chance of winning, and an 88 percent chance of not losing! When presented with this scenario, we had a total team buy-in!

At this point, it is important to introduce the importance of the formation that a coach employs as he sends ten players on the field. There are several traditional formations, such as the 4-4-2, which is 4 defenders, 4 midfielders and 2 attackers. There is also the 4-3-3, which is more offensive minded, while 4-5-1 is a defensive posture.

Here is the field, more commonly called "the pitch" and you can imagine those formations taking up their spaces in the back, middle and forward parts of the pitch.

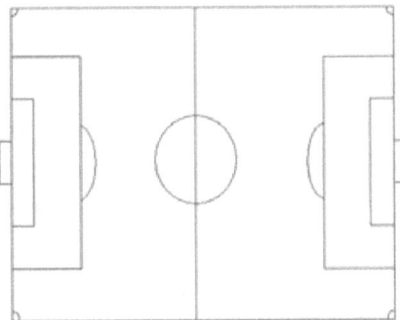

These are assigned positions with assigned territories and roles. A well-disciplined team will fill those spots and not leave their territories vacant. It is the culmination of the evolution of soccer, where kids played "swarm ball" versus pros playing in strict formation. So, a more well-disciplined, traditional team should beat a less disciplined, traditional team, if you are playing a traditionally disciplined game. But based on our team's agreement that we are playing a thirty-minute game and then a thirty-minute game, we are by no means playing a traditional game, and therefore discipline is not only not necessary, but probably hinders our effort.

But don't think throwing away discipline means we are willy-nilly leaving it up to chance. No, here is where we bring in math and biology and guile. Every team warms up in practice with a form of keep-away, where the players form a circle to pass the ball around, while two players in the middle run around trying to intercept the passes. But the players forming the circle use angles and superior numbers to keep the ball away. It is frustrating for those in the middle, but as a warm-up drill, it is highly effective at getting defenders and strikers ready to create an outnumbered situation in their favor during the game.

So, I posed to the team that for our thirty-minute game we need to outnumber our opponents. Again, agreement. Outnumbering your opponent in a portion of the field will lead to two benefits:

1. Ability to maintain possession while advancing
2. Ability to regain possession when the ball is lost

Now we have built enough successive agreement that we can use the power of agreement to replace an actual statistical number, because the exact number is not essential, and what is much more important is that we believe the number we agree upon. And considering the fact that we don't have time to do the research, this is the next best thing.

So, I asked "What is the chance that a player can move the ball forward when in a 1v1 situation?" The answers varied in range, but all were around a 50/50 chance. I made them agree on one number and it was a 55 percent chance of moving the ball forward. Is it that number? Who knows! But we agreed it was that number, so we were able to move on. Ok, what is the chance of moving forward in a 2v1 situation? (2 of our players vs 1 of theirs). Again the team shouted out numbers and we landed on 80 percent. I yelled, "Someone write these down" and took the momentum building to run through the other possible scenarios. The chances of moving forward in the following matchups were as follows:

1 v 1: 55 %
2 v 1: 80 %
2 v 2: 40 %
3 v 2: 70 %
3 v 1: 90 %
3 v 3: 45 %
4 v 3: 60 %
4 v 2: 80 %

All plausible numbers and that's really what counted here. Next was to look at how often we may encounter these matchups. I don't even know if the statistics exist, but again, we weren't going to do that research with our limited time. One player, I think it was Tom, pulled out his computer and created a little spreadsheet that we would need to track the numbers and also do some quick math to find the one number that can tell us our chance ... a weighted average! We agreed we would probably be evenly matched for 50 percent of the game and employ our outnumbered advantage strategy for the other half of the game. So here is the table of matchups and their chances of success, all calculated into a weighted average of a 51 percent success potential.

Offensive Situation	% Successful	% Encountered	Weighted Contribution
Evenly Matched	40%	50%	20%
5v4	52%	10%	5%
4v3	55%	10%	6%
3v2	60%	10%	6%
2v1	70%	5%	4%
5v3	70%	5%	4%
4v2	75%	5%	4%
3v1	80%	5%	4%
Chance of Success		100%	51%

One cool thing about calculating a weighted average (if there are any) is that you never know what the final number is going to be as you calculate the parts. It hits you as a surprise. In our case, based on all the numbers we agreed upon, the final chance of success for our strategy was 51 percent. At first, we all heard the number and were all not overly impressed. A bit of a silence ensued, and I was not really sure how to segue from here to other points I wanted to make.

Rescue was on its way! I could see Meegs looking at the team and seeing the momentum stalled in their mannerisms. Then the players started turning attention to Meegs and I'm sure he could feel it. He stands up and launches, "Guys, guys ... *at the beginning of practice today* we all were thinking we were gonna...what was it Coach? *"Lose but gain wisdom?"* and now we've got the makings of a plan to win!" The fact that he called me Coach sent an invisible message to the players instilling authority into my temporary role. I will be forever grateful for that move. As if to trip up his Belushi rally speech one of the players lobbed a bomb (which I hate to say was correct and could have blown our plan off the rails) by saying just loud enough for us all to hear, *"Meegs, we made all this shit up!"* Meegs earned his apparent logic stripes with his reply, which was immediate, *"It doesn't have to be exact! It just has to be believable!"*

There was stunned silence. I was impressed with Meegs. The team was impressed with Meegs. Meegs was impressed too with his own impromptu leadership and he owned it! He continued addressing his teammates, *"Do you believe that two players can get by 1 player 80 percent of the time? I do! Do you believe a 3 on 2 will be successful 60 percent of the time? I do!"* The players also screamed "Yes!" on that one with Meegs. *"Well hell,"* he continued, *"numbers don't lie, and our numbers tell us we got a 51% chance of winning and that's against a really good team! You know who likes a 51% advantage?"* Ok, now where the hell is he going with this I thought? *"Casinos! Casinos will be happy all day long to provide you booze, meals, and rooms just to take 1% of all the gambling!"* How he knew that at 17 years old we don't know but like Belushi, he was on a roll, and no one wanted to stop him. As Meegs inevitably started to crack up, the rest of the team caught immediate contagion and burst out laughing. Hell, they may have only been laughing at the moxie that Meegs showed with his quick and confident speech, but it didn't matter. As usual, you could choose from a buffet of reasons to laugh with or at Meegs. He didn't know it, but he had done just what I needed and couldn't do myself—he built a perfect segue. This is right where I wanted to be to introduce the larger strategy.

"Ok! Thank you, Meegs, for your heroics," I said. *"So, listen ... here's how we put this into action."*

What is the biggest obstacle to outnumbering your opponent? Staying in position.

What is the biggest obstacle to assisting teammates who are outnumbered? Staying in position. Traditional soccer stays in position. You hear it all the time when a coach or players yells, "Keep your shape!" Remember that phrase because we are going to use it to freeze the other team. So traditional, well-disciplined teams, like the one we will face in two days, have mastered the task of keeping their shape. They will stay spread out over the entire pitch. We are not going to keep our shape! Remember from biology there is a word for that … anyone?

Like an amoeba? Yes! Like kids playing swarm ball? Kind of? What's that word?

"Amorphous!" Yelled Zach. Yes! Amorphous is to be without shape. But what would you call it when you are without shape … on purpose? No answers.

"Not Amorphous … but BeMorphous!" I yell, and the players howled again. So, borrowing from Belushi myself, I continue. *"BeMorphous soccer doesn't 'Keep your shape!' BeMorphous soccer is being amorphous on purpose and that purpose is to take the shape that is necessary at a given moment to have a greater presence in that part of the pitch than your opponent. We will exploit the rigidity of traditional soccer formations by over-weighting our team's presence in a portion of the field to achieve and maintain the crucial advantage...a man advantage."* I go on to explain more of what it looks like.

BeMorphous soccer will actually punish opposing teams for doing the "right thing." In fact, it will be our players, the ones employing the BeMorphous approach on the other team, who yell to our teammates to "Keep your Shape!" while in fact not doing so. Just hearing someone yell "Keep your Shape!" will hit a nerve with the opponent and make them retreat to a portion of the pitch where they will not see the ball as we make small geometrical passes ever closer to the goal far away from the opponent who is diligently guarding his empty territory.

The other shape-freezing thing for us to yell will be for our defensive backs and keeper, who have a visual command of the entire field in front of them to yell "Switch it!" This is a command to send the ball from a congested side of the field over to an open player way on the other side, essentially rebalancing and redistributing the players across the pitch to follow the "switched" ball. This would redistribute opponent players away from the congested area where we have the ball. That would actually be reducing their presence and increasing our numerical advantage, all because they were doing the right thing!

Divide and Conquer the Field

Let's try to visualize this. Remember the diagram of the pitch above. The pitch is commonly divided into thirds when looking at the field lengthwise. Let's add the same concept widthwise and you have nine boxes. BeMorphous soccer creates the outnumbered advantage in four of the nine boxes, in the middle and forward third of the field, while staying in the middle and side of that area. This allows for short passing with less risk of losing passes. This also allows for the ball to be repossessed quickly if lost to the opponents in the BeMorphous area.

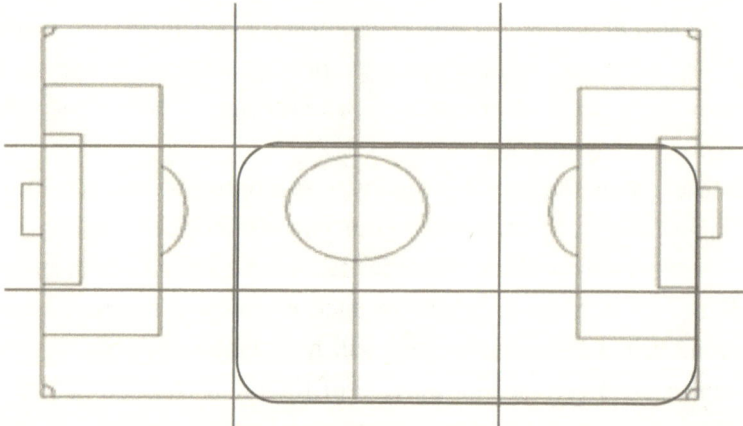

Even though by this time we had total team buy-in of the strategy, I offered what I believe to be a reasonable expectation on the result of this strategy; games would be won by scores of: 3-1, 4-1, 5-2, 6-2, 7-3. This unconventional offensive strategy will deliver more goals than traditional formations but will yield some goals on counterattacks. This relies on the huge advantage in a low-scoring sport in that the team with first lead wins 70 percent of the time. If done right, it is indefensible and the clearest proof that it is working would be a goal that is essentially walked into the net. Finally, because this strategy encourages players coming from far away positions to participate, almost everyone has a chance to score. This game could be incredibly fun—an experience the players will never forget!

The Last Practice

Our players were eager to get into our last practice after our serious non-practice strategy session the day before. I caught wind of some stories of good-natured banter and trash talk between our players and a couple of the alumnus on the college team. There were even bets on who buys lunch at Parma or Genoa Deli in town the next time they see each other over the holidays. They all played together for the same high school team a few years ago, so there was friendship in this "friendly" competition, especially with Joey, who helped Coach Bergen make this game possible. After all, he was the high school's leading scorer in his day and now was tearing it up in college. Our team was buoyed by our strategy and had good sport in their teasing, the kind that comes with a secret confidence. The college players returned fire in text messages with the vigor and confidence you'd expect from older, better players.

So, for our last practice, we went back to odd numbers. Not the 2 v 1 because that's basic. BeMorphous soccer will be played in traffic. We practiced 3 v 2, 4 v 3, 4 v 2, 3 v 1 because this will have us advance the ball in tight spaces. Halfway through this last practice, and when we all could see that a numerical advantage works, I called the team in. I had a pet peeve about soccer I wanted to share …. and again … use it to our advantage. Here is my gripe, and the solution I offered.

The Dreaded Own Goal

As a father of a goalkeeper, and one who played defense in my high school days, I appreciate what it takes for the back line and keeper to keep the ball out of the net. All that effort is pure of heart, but on occasion it results in a ball going in your net, not because of a tremendous, curving fire-blast from a talented striker, but sadly instead, a deflection off our own player. The dreaded "Own Goal." Ask any keeper what is the worst goal to concede and the Own Goal is first, just ahead of a pin-ball scramble cheap-shit goal.

The "Own Goal" should be eliminated from the sport of Futbol, for the same reason tonsils are taken out of a child ... they are useless! Tonsils can get infected, causing negative health effects which outweigh any benefit of their existence, if there even is benefit. The problem with the Own Goal is that while its benefit is also in question, it provides a double negative in its existence.

First, in defense of the defense. Futbol defenders work tirelessly tracking strikers who may be faster than them. Defenders steady themselves to not be faked out or nutmegged by the fancy skills of the strikers. And defenders throw their bodies into harm's way in a tackle, or a 50-50 header or just in the firing line of a blasted shot from close range. What does all that mean? It means that by definition and by paycheck, defenders are doing all they can do to keep the ball out of the net. If a ball goes in their own net that came off a defender's effort to clear it ... well, that hurts the defender bad enough. It goes without saying that it hurts the whole team. So, does it need to be pointed out even further by declaring that an Own Goal? I say no.

Now let's look at the striker. Every striker is there to score goals. It is the clearest form of merit-based evidence for a striker in their salary negotiations. How many goals they score is huge. Aside from the league recognition of most goals, like the Ballon d'Or (Golden Boot) a striker may score the most for their team that season, or the most in their team's history. It could just be an extremely important goal that won the title!

Imagine that taken away! This is the other side of the double negative. Imagine a subjective call on the pitch that determined the ball glanced off a defender who now is saddled with an Own Goal, while at the same time your striker is deprived of the glory of a goal counting toward their career tally. My point is that offensive players strive to put the ball in very "dangerous situations" that hope to end up with it in the back of the net. If it went in but not by a teammate completing the play, but by creating such a dangerous situation that the clearing attempt of the defender lands it in the net … chalk that goal up to the striker that whipped it in with such precision, spin, and intent. If it was a complete blunder with little or no offensive effort, then credit that goal to the Keeper on the offensive side. No more scoring upon yourself!

The Own Goal, as it is recognized in the English Premier League today, is not just a useless statistic, it actually hides the attention that should be given to the other team. Look up Own Goal as a statistic in the EPL. There were about 25 of them last season and they are widely spread across defenders on every team. They are not concentrated on one or two players. Any defender can mistakenly deflect a ball in the net in the heat, and speed, of the action. These players are merely tagged with the effect of an own goal, not the causation. The better questions that could be answered by an Own Goal statistic are:

"What **Team** is **Causing** the most own goals?"
"Which **Offensive Players** are **Creating** dangerous passes that result in Own Goals?"

Guess what? You can't find those answers because the Own Goal statistic is looking in the opposite direction! It seeks to punish, where no punishment is due, instead of rewarding the type of play you want to incentivize, which now goes unrecognized. I will bet a round of pints at an Everton Pub that Own Goal creation IS concentrated on a few teams and a handful of players. Everton had a young Spaniard for a few seasons named Gerard Deulofeu who exemplified what I mean by sending in crosses that were dangerous. Often, he hit the ball with topspin and pace that made it bounce before the keeper could get it. The ball was filled with energy from his pass such that it only required a slight touch of a player's boot to deflect and redirect the ball in an unsavable direction. That boot could be a teammate's, which makes the play look brilliant. The teammate gets the goal and Deulofeu gets the assist. All proper recognition. Or that redirection could easily be a defender's attempt to clear the ball out of danger, but in that split second, the ball is sent flying into the roof of the net. The defender is saddled with the own goal and Gerard gets no recognition for his skill. It was an offensive threat that caused the goal, not a defensive blunder. So, let's just do away with the Own Goal soon!

But … until that happens … let's ask one more question.
Can we **Intentionally Cause** an own goal?

Another problem with Own Goals as currently treated is that they are an afterthought, a random act that befalls upon a team like other bad luck such as lightning striking a tree and it falls on your car. The responsibility is dismissed with the own goal as if it is merely an act of God. It is not, it is an act of men—men like Gerard. So how can we build in chances for an own goal happening in our favor? You can't really do that in run of play. While the ball is moving between players and up the field, the organic nature of the game has the chances to score or create an own goal situation built into the game. There is not much influence that can be applied while the ball is moving. But when the ball stops … that's where there are choices and strategies honed on the training pitch that can be employed. When there is a foul called giving your team a free kick in a distance short enough to put the ball on net, but too far to be a realistic shot, you want to send it into a dangerous area. That is around the six-yard box.

Own Goal Strategy

An established part of the game of soccer is drawing a foul. Sure, the people who don't see soccer as the beautiful game may criticize when players roll on the ground in agony after getting a bump. It is part theatrics. That's why it is called "drawing" a foul. The foul is the desired outcome of intentionally creating contact that is or looks to be a foul. And just a note to the people who hate that part, the rules do allow a Referee to call the foul on the player trying to draw the foul if there really was no foul at all. I love what they call that infraction … the foul would be for "Simulation." It is more commonly known as "taking a dive" but leave it to the Brits to dress it up in eloquent language. So, the pitch is not a place for complete actors, but there is room for those who can exaggerate. The strategy starts by drawing fouls, lots of them, in the first part of their half of the pitch. See the following illustrations.

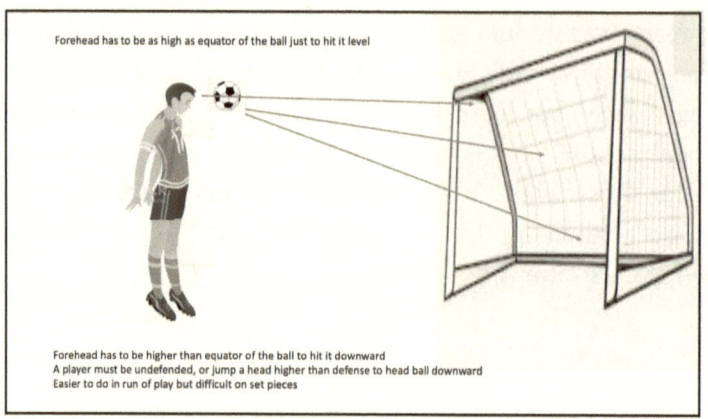

Forehead has to be as high as equator of the ball just to hit it level

Forehead has to be higher than equator of the ball to hit it downward
A player must be undefended, or jump a head higher than defense to head ball downward
Easier to do in run of play but difficult on set pieces

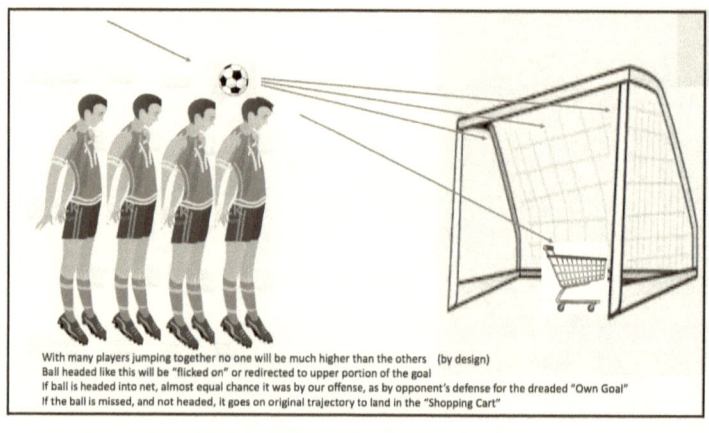

With many players jumping together no one will be much higher than the others   (by design)
Ball headed like this will be "flicked on" or redirected to upper portion of the goal
If ball is headed into net, almost equal chance it was by our offense, as by opponent's defense for the dreaded "Own Goal"
If the ball is missed, and not headed, it goes on original trajectory to land in the "Shopping Cart"

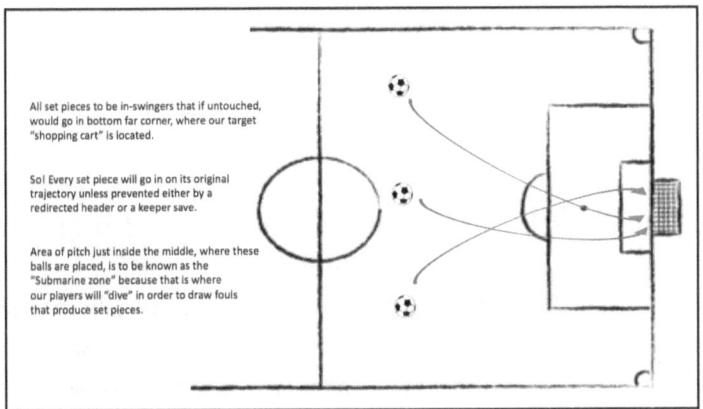

All set pieces to be in-swingers that if untouched, would go in bottom far corner, where our target "shopping cart" is located.

So! Every set piece will go in on its original trajectory unless prevented either by a redirected header or a keeper save.

Area of pitch just inside the middle, where these balls are placed, is to be known as the "Submarine zone" because that is where our players will "dive" in order to draw fouls that produce set pieces.

The general idea is...

- All free kicks are inswingers on net, outswingers end up missing net
- Target bottom corner but headable around 6-10 yards out— land it in "shopping cart"
- Stack players close together, creating a landing strip for the ball
- Opponents will crowd the same area, increasing chance the ball will be redirected
- In a crowd like this, all heads will be around the same height
- For a player to head the ball downward they have to be higher than the ball
- This is a flick, a redirection using the ball's kicked energy, not the header's energy
- Why? Top of players heads doesn't require head to be equally as high as the ball
- This lets the entire pack of players be capable of skimming the ball toward net
- Requires the keeper to protect two paths at once
- The original flight path and the skimmed redirection

Sounds crazy, but this too was well embraced by the team. We were deploying secret, untested weapons, believing they will work. Those are dangerous ingredients.

The Game

It was a brisk and sunny afternoon when the college team bus pulled into Tiger Hollow, as our high school's field is known. Set down in a valley, it is a great amphitheater for sporting battles. The last advice I gave the team was to start the game normally for the first ten minutes. Play your positions wide across the whole width of the field so that they see us wide and therefore expect us to be wide. You can't catch them off guard if you start with the trap sprung. It will be a risk to our whole score-first plan, but it will give us the best chances to make them feel out of sorts when we deploy the BeMorphous strategy. Plus, teams take a few minutes to get settled into the game.

The game begins and there is a bit of nervousness on our side, not from the fact that they are playing a much bigger and better team, but more from trying to play while keeping a secret. The opponents close down on our possession quickly, making it difficult to string passes together as we played in all nine boxes of the pitch. We did, however, plant the seeds of the trap by switching the ball wide to our player who is keeping their shape, after yelling for the ball to be switched wide, while our team kept its shape. This signaled to our opponents that we would actually do what we are instructing our team to do.

While not very pretty, our style of play that first ten minutes was able to disrupt their effort to play a controlled possession attack by tackling well and kicking it long back into their defensive zone. However, it was tough to defend against their sheer physical size and strength advantage.

At eight minutes in they sent a long ball, which was deftly headed by their striker, to an overlapping winger who cut his run from down the side towards the middle where he had time to line up his shot from twenty yards out. This ball had bad intentions as it curled towards the back post, top corner, until Nick got fingertips on the ball just barely sending it over goal. That ball, while in the air, was the complete destruction of our plan.

As Mike Tyson once said, *"Everyone has a plan until they get punched."* Well, we dodged that first punch and made it past the ten minute mark without conceding a goal. We survive Phase 1, and the trap had been set.

Now we start playing without shape on purpose, as we take the ball up the right side. Our center and left midfielder pinch into the right side of the field and string together a bunch of tight passes. It creates our first penetration into their last third, resulting in a nice through pass to our striker who almost chased it down for an open chance on goal. Instead, it was a tad bit heavy and rolled out for a goal kick. While the significance of this possession went unnoticed to the opponent's team, I could see in the boys' faces as they trotted back to position for the goal kick that they knew BeMorphous worked!

After a few minutes of trading possession, we attempted another long ball, but this was easily gathered up by their keeper, but instead of hurrying back to positions our team is still in the opponent's half as the keeper rolls the ball to their defender to start their possession up field. Skilled teams do this with geometric precision, as they complete a bunch of passes that are like the sides of squares and triangles. They are usually able to do that as their midfielders drop back to help, typically outnumbering the offense of the other team. But we had good numbers of players in the area they tried to pass through. When in their first two to three passes we almost got to the ball, more of our players crept closer to the action, after, of course, yelling "Keep your shape!" The college team, hearing our call to our own team to essentially spread out, gave them the determination to stay the course of trying to pass their way out from the back. Remember, BeMorphous is not just an offensive strategy ... it is a means of retaking possession quickly as well.

The next several passes didn't move the ball forward and barely had them maintain possession. At last, while one of their players hurried their next pass, one of our players cut it off from the intended recipient. Now we were stringing together short passes while they became frustrated at the number of players we had in the area. I know we had one defender all the way up there as I saw Cass be an outlet and move the ball to Adam, who was now more in the middle, creating a two on one situation where a beautiful give and go between Adam and Dean gave Adam an open shot from fifteen feet out. Adam's shot was not the high blasting shot that often makes highlight reels, but rather a more effective shot that looked like another pass in our string of passes. The ball rolled with pace along the ground just inside the left post. GOAL! First Goal! At twenty three minutes into the game, we had the lead!

Seeing so many of our players, including defenders, up on offense gave all the players a sense of "Hey, what are you doing here?" but our team's answer is with delight, while their team's answer is with pure frustration.

Play resumes and after that there was a battle for the ball just past midfield and the college team won possession. They move it out wide; we spread out to recover, dissolving back to disciplined formation. After some probing passes around a perimeter some twenty five yards out, Tyler anticipates their next pass and intercepts. Shielding the opponent from the ball, Tyler is able to pass a short way back to Sam, who, facing up field, could see Bonnie getting ready to run. The pass back was a perfect slow roller that Sam blasted over the top of the college defenders.

Bonnie took off but so did several of our other strikers and midfielders! Bonnie outran the defender to take control of the ball but could not continue the run as two defenders had caught up and took defensive positions. Usually, a long ball over the top finds the striker outnumbered, and it is difficult to keep possession, much less advance the ball. This time Bonnie had an outlet sideways to Dean on an overlapping run, which moved the ball forward and cutting in towards the goal. Dean could see two orange jerseys and hit Adam on a cutback pass. Adam faked the shot, wrong-footing the defense and the keeper, as they fully expected that shot. Instead, he rolled it sideways to Killian, cutting in front of his defender where Killian side-footed the ball three feet inside the left post, halfway between the ground and crossbar! 2-0 at thirty five minutes into the game!

Joy and laughter on our side, serious questioning and gesturing on their side. Whose guy was that?

My younger son John, a very skilled striker himself, was in the stands and started blasting out text messages to all his friends and very quickly, the bleachers started filling up. Even Coach Bergen was alerted to the events. This has gone from what was really just another practice game to a full-on event! Tons of students fill the stands and not all who regularly attended their home games. It was a beautiful fall Friday afternoon made for a great show building up and attendance kept growing.

While everything seemed to be working well, suddenly reality crashed the scene. We tried once again to crowd in as they took the ball out from goal with a few passes in one corner of the pitch. As we yelled "Keep your shape" while at the same time doing the opposite by compressing in toward the ball, they yelled "switch it" and did so. The fatal underbelly of BeMorphous soccer was exposed. With a mighty boot, they crossed the ball out of congestion to their players who had maintained their shape. We had vacated that area of the pitch so they were able to break towards the goal across midfield. They may have had a 4 on 2, but surely, they had 3 vs 2 as they approached the box. Joey dribbled in and sent a no-look pass to the side, as if he had done that a thousand times before. It made his teammate look great as all he had to do was slot it right as Nick had chosen the other outlet to defend. Mind you, this takes place in seconds. Easy to question after viewing slow motion replays but be the one on the pitch and your decision making operates in split seconds. So, it is 2-1 at thirty six minutes and we hold on after that body blow to get to halftime.

Halftime Speech?

You never want to head into the locker at halftime with the opponent having just scored. It sticks on you like a bad aroma. A goal against you changes what you want to say to your players at the last minute. But this time, things were different. Our boys didn't take that last goal harshly. It was expected and the huge counterattack they mustered was excusable. All our boys wanted to do was get to the locker where they could talk about what took place in the first half, and how the crowd was growing! Actually, I had no half time pep talk ready. I had done all my speech making in order to get to this game. Everything in my head was about what could happen ... now was the time to let the players talk about what did happen. I think the average of what the players said when in the locker room was "Holy shit" followed by "Did you see ..." "Was that you I passed to?" and "Can you believe?"

With only a few moments left before leaving the locker room, I asked the team to focus up. All I said was, *"You won the most important game ... the 30-minute game. And you brought the ship home with a lead at the half. Now the odds favor us! Play your asses off this half!"*

Okay, that's not up there with Vince Lombardi, but all I wanted to do was remind them of the odds that we created. The odds that, if we believe them, will give us the advantage we need.

The second half starts, and we are playing with good energy, fueled by the crowd. We make one or two offensive efforts with a shot just over goal, but really the second half settles into the boys just hanging on for dear life. We all know it. We are, by design, not playing BeMorphous as you can't employ that strategy all game. We are playing to try to hold the lead given to us from the BeMorphous strategy. At seventy five minutes the opponent's discipline and physical advantage were showing. They were winning 50-50 balls and bodying our players off the ball. They passed the ball from their back line with the geometry of triangles and squares. Advancing through midfield, the geometry turned more to choreography as their players moved toward the pass, deflecting the ball to a close-by teammate on their own path to open space down the side. A quick give-and-go sent the winger across the top of the box. Our defender closed the gap by moving out from the center. The winger side foots a rolling pass near the center top of the box; midfielder sees his shot may be blocked, so he whiffs on his attempt on purpose! This is called "Dummying" the ball. His fake kick let the ball continue through and find the feet of Joey with time to first nudge the ball to his favored foot and then launching a knuckling, rising fire blast of a shot just past Nick's fingers into the top far corner. The score is now 2-2 with eight minutes to go! That shot was such a treat to watch. I'm sure for Joey it was too, as he had many of those when playing here for the high school, and probably accepted that upon graduation he had hit his last great shot here at Tiger Hollow in any meaningful competition. This blast was icing on the cake.

At the eighty seventh minute the ref blows his whistle. Foul! Was it a dive? Who knows, but it gets awarded to us. Twenty five yards out and over on the right side if facing the goal. Killian, our lefty, stands above the ball. Defensive line is back enough that it would take very little time for five or six of our players to run in and set up together ten yards from the far post of the goal. Since we are concentrated in the same area so is their defense. That is what we wanted. It seemed like half the players on the field were all packed in together, looking for Killian's kick, which had height and curve. It had topspin and side spin, too. The ball just looked from the beginning like a "dangerous" ball.

Nobody can tell you what specifically happened, but with certainty the ball ended up in the net! The ball appeared to be headed just inside the post, but it was deflected by the group of players all jumping together. Was their pushing and shoving? Sure. Was there shirt-pulling? Sure. But there was no whistle on play. The only uncertainty was who scored.

That sure as hell didn't matter at the time because we had to close out the final three minutes. The boys did so by clearing the ball as far and as high as they possibly could, even into the bleachers, which got the fans crazed. With the final whistle, our bench poured onto the field; the student fans did as well, and so did the opposing team, as they reluctantly acknowledged that they were part of a great match played, a great chapter in Ridgefield soccer history.

Meegs celebrating a teammate's goal and sharing his enthusiasm with the home crowd.
Meegs never needed it to be about his own accomplishment to celebrate.
He is the consummate team player.

In my post-match pep talk, just before sending them home, I had to ask. *"Which one of you scored that last goal?"* Any player would like to have the credit for that last goal to stay with them as the story is told and retold, but no one jumped to own it. One said "I was near where it came down but I didn't feel the ball." Another said, "I didn't get ball, but I definitely cracked heads with someone!" Some laughs and then quiet as we waited for someone else ... but nothing else came.

I took the moment of hesitation as my chance to reframe the narrative of the own goal to something positive. I yelled "You guys scored the own goal! We did it!! The hell with luck. The hell with serendipity! We created our own, own goal!"

Handing the Keys Back

Coach Bergen returned for practice that next Monday with the state tourney starting later that week. I met him in front of the assembled team. Everyone was smiling and about to burst with energy from the victory and the anticipation of Coach's reaction. They were all waiting for that trigger. I was even smirking as I handed Coach my whistle and clip board. Coach too was grinning as he ignited the fireworks with one question: *"What the hell just happened here?"*

For the next hour, it was just the boys telling Coach Bergen about every play, every highlight, in between laughs. Coach rattled off questions: *"What's the deal with Keep your shape?" "What the hell is B-Murphy soccer?"* and *"Who is kicking the ball in shopping carts?"* And *"Are you telling me you MADE them score an own goal for us????"*

After great stories and laughs, Coach Bergen did what Coach Bergen does well—he got the boys back into a disciplined soccer practice. The kind where keeping your shape means staying in your position. The boys just seemed to have a great energy about them. Coach Bergen harnessed and focused that energy throughout the state championship. The boys did not lose one home game that season and went on to become state champions! The final game was against the perennial powerhouse and major rival Glastonbury, which ended in an overtime draw. There were no penalty kicks to settle the draw, so each team was co-state champions for that year. A different, and perhaps less fulfilling ending, but over the years, the sound of State Champions sounds just as sweet no matter how it ended.

Oh, and remember the logo with the three stars on the warmup sweats? That was the first year that logo was worn. Well, that gear became collector's items as the next year the new logo added another star to represent the fourth state championship!

~

Someone asked, can BeMorphous strategy be applied to other sports? Yes, I suppose so. The best example was Derek Jeter, shortstop for the NY Yankees, taking a cut-off throw from the outfielder that went near the first base dugout and throwing the runner out at the plate! If Jeter had "Kept his shape" he never would have made the play. Jeter played without shape. He was amorphous, on purpose! He was BeMorphous!

So, an element of this story sits on the dividing line between the book I am honoring and the book I am writing. Everything else in this book is harmless through and through. But this story has an element that crosses the line.

In this book, *Apparent Logic,* this story is a great example of weaving various ingredients which are not facts but merely happy replacements for those facts to get a reader to think like I do, that this could happen.

On the other hand, the story as truth, and the gambit of yelling "Keep your shape" not only pays tribute to Stephen Potter's Gamesmanship, it perfectly exemplifies it. I couldn't be more proud. For you see, if you just take it as the happy to be told story, it is harmless. But if you really analyze the beauty in the "Keep your shape" ploy, it is pure chicanery, meant to game your opponent. It is meant to gain advantage, while apparent logic only wants to create equal company.

Finally, with this story more than others, I feel a need to divulge where the story deviates from the truth ... if, in fact, it deviates from the truth at all. I will resist that need but let me help a little. The parts about the logo and winning the fourth state championship are true. You can decide for yourself on the rest.

If you are involved at all with the Everton Football Club, or if you are Ryan Reynolds or Rob McElhenney, owners of the Wrexham AFC team, I would be happy to share more details on BeMorphous soccer and the Own Goal strategy to contribute to your team's success!

That offer also stands for the Greenville Triumph, David Beckham's new Inter Miami CF, Millwall FC, any National Team, The Everton affiliated youth teams here in CT. I think you get the idea. Let's make this happen for you!

CHAPTER XI

SKIERS HAVE HIJACKED OUR CALENDAR! IT'S BEEN ALL DOWNHILL FROM THERE!

efore we jump into the calendar controversy, let's ground ourselves in the power of the behind-the-scenes administrative state, and the capacity of the individual to make a significant act. An act that is accepted at the time at face value, but the significance grows with each passing day like a cancer metastasizing. The fallout growing increasingly annoying as the realization that it was all preventable in the first place.

Where do you live? We recite the answer starting specific, then panning out to a more general location, only to then jump backwards to add another level of specificity. I grew up at:

10 Roosevelt Ave, Larchmont, NY 10538

That is a specific house, on a street of which there are many, in my town, of which there are many in my state. Then we jump backward to add a Zip Code, which divides towns into regions. Why do we do it this way? Because states go back hundreds of years and streets and towns go back even further. It wasn't until 1963 that the US Postal Service introduced the Zip Code system, so the most recent part of your address gets added on at the end. Makes sense? Yes.

So in 1963, this Zip Code was introduced and a method of assigning these wonderful five-digit numbers was devised. There was plenty going on in our country to keep attentions riveted, such as ending the Vietnam War, putting a man on the moon, burning bras, and smoking dope. Do you think anyone cared about how zip codes were going to be distributed?

Hell no! Well … actually, hell yeah … there were two people.

They were both back-office town administrators with such mundane responsibilities as logging home sales, approving permits and collecting your taxes. But these two went way above the call of duty to leave an indelible mark of significance for their towns in perpetuity.

The first clerk, and she should rightly be called "the First Enterprising Clerk," travelled all the way from Dillingham, Alaska to request, successfully, the Zip Code 00001 for their town! Why Dillingham? No reason but for the heroics of the First Enterprising Clerk.

Now I think an argument could be made (remember, the purpose of this book is to make compelling arguments so I will always think and argument can be made) that the town of Lubec, Maine, should have gotten the Zip Code of 00001 since the rising sun hits land in the USA on the shores of Lubec, Maine, first! Apparently, there is at least some logic to that argument.

Let's move to the story of the other clerk. We will call him the Other Enterprising Clerk since it doesn't matter that he wasn't first in the nation to reserve a specific zip code. No, for him, it only mattered that he beat his two neighbors.

Where was the *"Shot Heard Round the World?"* Where is the birthplace of the Revolution? A young lad overheard the British forces scheming in the Green Dragon Tavern (still serving pints to Patriots in downtown Boston) and tipped off Paul Revere. Everyone knows the midnight ride of Paul Revere in 1776, alerting Patriots that the British forces were headed to Lexington and Concord, Massachusetts. There, their plans of confiscating and destroying the Patriot's weapons and ammunition stockpiles were thwarted. Blood was spilled on the bridge and the first battle of the Revolution had begun.

Fast forward to 1963. What town has the zip code 01776? Sudbury!

The neighboring town to Concord and Lexington. The home of my oldest son's birth. And, apparently, the home of "the Other Enterprising Clerk." This clerk got that zip code when nobody was looking. Was he helped with a handshake deal in the smoke-filled back room of the Green Dragon Tavern between some Sudbury muckity-mucks and a postal service rouge agent? That secret remains untold. It is possible the Sudbury clerk didn't even need to make the argument, but if he had to, it may have been built upon the fact that Sudbury sent many of the soldiers who fought at Lexington and Concord. Regardless, 01776 is Sudbury, and the bitterness between the towns grows to this day!

So now that we are armed with the knowledge of the power of the unseen back office administrative bureaucrats, let's turn our attention to our holiday calendar and when our holidays were created. Here is 2024.

Date	Holiday	Year Added
Monday, January 01	New Year's Day	1870
Monday, January 15	Martin Luther King, Jr. Day	1983
Monday, February 19	Washington's Birthday	1879
Monday, May 27	Memorial Day	1888
Wednesday, June 19	Juneteenth Day	2021
Thursday, July 04	Independence Day	1870
Monday, September 02	Labor Day	1894
Monday, October 14	Columbus Day	1968
Monday, November 11	Veterans Day	1954
Thursday, November 28	Thanksgiving Day	1870
Wednesday, December 25	Christmas Day	1870

I know … right? What a total mess! How did we let it get this way? There are three months with no federal holiday, March and April, which is understandable as they fall right when we should be in a good work and school groove. You know … nose to the grindstone mentality as the weather turns from unusable to barely tolerable. So, March and April don't need to be rescued. But August? Who the hell was representing August since 1870 when our first holidays were created? Nothing? Hello!! Nice sunny summer weather? Anybody? How the hell did August come up short?

Because we let "Big Snow" hijack the holiday calendar!

For perspective, let's look again at this holiday calendar and how different constituents are served by these days off.

Date	Holiday	Skiers	Family Summer Vacation	Northeast Fishing
Monday, January 01	New Year's Day	1		
Monday, January 15	Martin Luther King, Jr. Day	1		
Monday, February 19	Washington's Birthday	1		
Monday, May 27	Memorial Day			
Wednesday, June 19	Juneteenth Day		1	
Thursday, July 04	Independence Day		1	
Monday, September 02	Labor Day		1	1
Monday, October 14	Columbus Day			1
Monday, November 11	Veterans Day	1		1
Thursday, November 28	Thanksgiving Day	1		
Wednesday, December 25	Christmas Day	1		
		6	3	3

Now ... what has been hidden in plain sight is revealed to those who look but don't see. The skiers have hijacked the holiday calendar, and we want it back!

We see that the skiers have managed to amass six of the eleven holidays into their ski season.

Our poor families, who are the backbone of our population, have all taken part in the summer vacation ritual, yet only have three holidays! And that's being generous because, as we look a little deeper, we only got Juneteenth recently.

And selfishly, (I liked that I used the word "fish" in selfishly) as a New Englander I want more holidays in the Autumn when the Striped Bass are migrating south to the Chesapeake Bay. But that's just me.

You may enjoy winter sports and be saying there is nothing to see here, but when we look a little deeper at when these holidays were created, there are things that are harder to explain. We start with the original four in 1870. Working backwards, you have Christmas, Thanksgiving, and Independence Day. Those make sense. But why New Year's Day? Remember, we are talking about the Industrial Revolution and the Birth of a Nation. Nothing says we are an unstoppable industrial force as much as grinding the gears of industry to a halt so we can rest, relax, and recover on the first working day of the year! How did that happen? I suspected Big Snow was behind it, but that will be proven out later.

Not long after, in 1879, it made sense to recognize Washington's contribution with a holiday and as this was the first holiday to be recognized for an individual human, the administrative clerks had to decide how to place it on the calendar. It could have been placed mid-year to commemorate any of General Washington's great victories in battle. It could have been placed on April 30th, the day he became our first President, but no ... it was decided to attach it to his birthday in February. As far as I know, General Washington hadn't accomplished that much on his first day on earth, so why recognize that? "Big Snow" once again. Now Big Snow has Christmas, New Years, and Washington's birthday! That's three of the five for the winter enthusiasts!

Then comes Memorial Day, recognized in 1888 because they realized that all soldiers deserved attention and that since March and April didn't have a holiday, May had to have one. Fair enough.

Six years later and we were in full Industrial Revolution mode and the people said, "We need recognition for the work we did to help our soldiers win the war." So, they created Labor Day in September. Perhaps this was the first indication that they knew the winter enthusiasts had control of the calendar and our administrative hero clerk at the time pushed the placement of Labor Day to September. This was significant because it was a holiday with no natural tether to a date on the calendar. It could have gone anywhere. Little did they know that their intention to make this a family summer holiday would get thwarted 100 years later as they changed the meaning of summer by changing the school calendar and starting school before Labor Day. As I said, who was representing August? Who was there to grease palms and keep school out of August?

Then, after fighting enough wars, admirably, it was decided in 1954 to complement Memorial Day, for those deceased soldiers, with Veteran's Day, for those alive with us today. Well deserved. But why November 11th? This recognized the day that World War 1 was ended some thirty six years earlier. All good intent but just to note, there are other days of significance in our military history.

Remember, each of these federal holidays fell onto the calendar without regard to how each would shape the entire holiday calendar. Sure, each one had a reason to exist on certain dates, but not all were rock solid in the reasoning for that date. Linking the recognition of a person's great accomplishments to their birth date is, in my opinion, a very weak link.

Let's now look at the last three federal holidays added to our calendar. Well, we wouldn't be celebrating holidays here in the USA unless a brave navigator named Christopher Columbus sailed the ocean blue in 1492 and discovered America. In 1971, this was added as a federal holiday falling on the second Monday of October, which occasionally falls on the anniversary of Columbus landing on October 12th. A worthy reason for the date, but wait ... "second Monday of October?" Now we are de-linking the celebration from a specific date. Interesting. Hold that thought.

In 1983, a holiday was added to recognize the great civil rights leader Martin Luther King, and the decision was made to have that fall on the third Monday of January, which would occasionally be his birthdate of January 15th. Wait a minute, now we are just approximating our days of recognition and celebration? Well, if that's the case …. I digress; let's finish the calendar.

The last and most recent holiday added to the federal calendar is June 19th, now known as Juneteenth, or Freedom Day. Officially recognized in 2021, this holiday is the oldest nationally celebrated commemoration of the ending of slavery in the United States. June 19, 1865, was the day news of the civil war ending had reached Texas and that all slaves were declared free. So, by comparison to other holidays, this one has a strong reason for the date.

In total, our holiday calendar is a mess. Each placed on the calendar without regard to the others. Each influenced by the powers that be at the time. We have four added since 1954 and half of those fell into the skiers portion of the calendar. Hmmm, what was going on back then?

When did skiing become a thing? One way to answer that is to look at when these winter sports meccas came into existence.

Vail	1966
Stratton	1961
Mt Snow	1954
Okemo	1955
Hunter	1960
Snowbird	1971
Aspen	1946
Killington	1958
Average	1959

So, we have all this ski industry activity taking place in the 50s and 60s ... why would that be? Well, they already had an unwarranted large share of the holiday schedule and knew they could use their influence to favor their industry as new holidays were placed on the calendar. How did they know that? A big piece of evidence is that nobody was sticking up for August!

Where was Major League Baseball pushing for a National Pastime holiday in August? Oh ... that's right, they were too busy celebrating victories without shaking hands. Meanwhile ski industry execs were being courted to Mt. Washington Hotel and other mountaintop chalets for secret holiday calendar planning meetings with cigars and brandy in the hot tub. That's how we ended up with this mess.

Now let's fix this using logic, precedence, de-linking and respect. Let's balance the calendar and give warm weather enthusiasts some more time outdoors to enjoy their activities.

We start at the beginning of the year, where we have three holidays in six weeks. We de-link the celebration of Martin Luther King Day from his approximate birth date and move it to honor his great civil rights accomplishments. We honor MLK by linking his recognition to the day that better represents his message. We move MLK Day to the first Tuesday in November, Election Day. This honors and respects MLK Day but doesn't help balance the calendar; it trades one ski holiday for another. It also creates another imbalance with Veteran's

Day occurring the next week in November. But it also creates opportunity.

Do you know that there are three days of recognition for military events in August? They are not holidays but significant days, nonetheless. August 4th, the day we commemorate Purple Heart Day, to honor all those injured in military service. What better way to enhance and expand that day of recognition than to move Veterans Day to August 4th!

There is an expression that describes a soldier's sacrifice that goes, "All gave some … some gave all." Combining Veterans Day with Purple Heart Day is with complete respect to the idea that every soldier makes a sacrifice, some singled out with a Purple Heart and the others with unrecognized wounds.

Now we have a federal holiday in August! At your backyard barbeque, we can all take a moment to raise a glass to and with our military heroes.

Finally, since we are on a roll and have good momentum, let's look at a huge date on our calendar that is not a federal holiday. Since we have precedence about de-linking a celebration from a specific date, there is an obvious place to apply this new standard. From now on Halloween will be on the last Saturday in October! No more rushing home from work on a rainy Tuesday to greet trick or treaters arriving in the dark. Just think of this idea from a safety standpoint. Being able to have Halloween strolls and parties while it is still light out will make a much safer experience. Halloween is also a huge young adult party night so they can all nurse their hangovers on Sunday instead of being groggy at work the next day. It is already a huge spending holiday as Americans dropped $12 billion to decorate and have scary fun in 2023. This would increase if Halloween were moved to Saturday. So, pick your reason to agree, they are all good ones!

Let's not be scared now. We just saved Halloween. A few simple, logical, respectful moves and we have a much better Holiday calendar. Sorry Skiers, but someone had to champion August!

I leave it to the next practitioner of Apparent Logic to tell the story of why April needs a holiday! Please publish that effort on the first day of April!

How does this story fare as an example of what we espouse?

Did the Ski industry really infiltrate the corridors of influence to load up holidays in winter months? The results cast a long shadow of suspicion; wouldn't you say?

And perhaps this little leading question ... the "Wouldn't you say?" is the diamond in the rough. First, because it is a nod to Potter and the Brits who often ask you to agree to an assertion or observation as if your permission is required. Like *"He really got 'em good with that story, didnee?"* Yes, "Didnee" really is one word when properly slapped on the end.

Second, that question leads you, nearly compelling you to agree. The story created the words and put them in your mouth. The story makes a compelling argument without the necessary ingredients. But it gets you to agree. That's the whole point, right there.

The story gives you enough ammo and the compunction to rush into your town's hall and make the case for August! And for April! This calamitous calendar mistake must not stand! We have lit the fuse and can now stand back to see the fireworks others will ignite with their newfound logic ... Apparent Logic.

CHAPTER XII

TOILET PAPER ... OVER OR UNDER?

It amazes me that this simple one or the other answer has not been solved as of this writing. I'm sure it has been tackled in every Miss Manners' column. I have never heard a legitimate reason for installing toilet paper so that it feeds off the roll from the bottom. I have also never sought out that argument, so it is possible it exists. However, I can put the whole thing to rest.

This matter was settled in the Roaring 20s in Newport, Rhode Island. Yes, before social media, the roll of toilet paper was anticipated in Newport, where the upper crust played lawn tennis and built sand-castles ... and built real castles!

As one Baron outdid the next with the expansive and historic architecture, combined with extremely lavish interior design, you can imagine that no expense was spared in the loo, the powder-room, the hopper. Fine Italian marble was everywhere. The finest porcelain. Gold-plated fixtures along with finely crafted mirrors.

That was the habitat we would find these profusely dressed, and utterly blinged-out women as they "powdered their noses." Imagine ... one of these Grande Dames reaching for a bunch of toilet paper.

The roll that was installed to feed from the bottom lays flatly against the wall. You remember the bathroom wall is made of the finest marble. As her hand reaches to gather the paper ... the diamonds and rubies and emeralds all scrape against the marble wall! Unacceptable!

Now, when correctly reversed, the toilet paper feeds out over the top of the roll, away from the wall. This is called a brilliant design. The whole intent of this brilliant design is completely lost by a care-less, thoughtless act of installing the TP with the roll feeding out from the bottom.

I feel if more people knew this bit of history, then we would never waste another moment on this subject and we can all get back to the task at hand, whatever that may be.

~

Let's run this story through a simple Apparent Logic filter …

Is the story true?
Is it a lie?
Does it get you to where you now have an answer to the age-old question?
Does it hurt anyone?
Is it better than no answer?
Can you voice it with authority?
Right ….?

A simple answer just as good at the correct answer, which, as we know, seems to be elusive. So this short little story is a gift to the world in that it takes one perplexing mystery off their minds. All that benefit in one page of effort … not bad!

CHAPTER XIII

THE OTHER A.D.D.

I couldn't believe it. Imagine walking into your therapist's office after many, many sessions and ... finally learning what is wrong with you? All those times on the couch ...

"I felt all flushed with fever, embarrassed by the crowd,
I felt she'd found my letters and read each one aloud..."

No but seriously, I value the feedback from therapy and my several therapists' depth of experience. I'm sure they read all the textbooks on every clinical condition so that when they reach consensus that I have something ... well then yes, I have something. Once you are told what you have, you can move on to what treatment there is for what you have.

Reminds me of a joke I'd like to share here.

==================================

An old man, a disheveled old man, walks into the bar at the Four Seasons Hotel. The bartender is crisply dressed, in his vest and tie, and also with a suspicious eye on the old man. The old man leans against the bar, looks at the bartender and in a soft but certain voice he says:

"I will have 4 glasses of your finest brandy."

With that request hanging in the air, and now a much quieter group of patrons at the bar, the bartender weighs his options and decides to get past the old man's looks and honor his request. As he pours the four

glasses of brandy, the patrons go back to their own business. That is
... until a moment later when this scene unfolds ...

The old man takes the first glass and gulps it straight down. He
quickly follows that by downing the second glass as the bartender
raises his voice. "Hey ... excuse me ..." but the old man doesn't
acknowledge his presence as the third glass is poured straight down
his throat. The bartender gently places his hand on the old man's arm
to gain his attention. *"Sir ... that is the finest brandy ... it is meant to be
sipped ... not gulped down ..."* The old man shakes his disheveled
assembly of clothes, looks at the bartender and stuns the patrons
when he announces ...

*"Sir ... you would drink this brandy the way I do too ... if you had what I
have ..."*

Total silence. The entire bar, filled with its assorted and eclectic
clientele, is glued to this emerging drama. Now, with the weight of the
combined audience, and with the confidence of thirty-years bartender
experience ... the bartender fills the void with the right question.

"So .... What do you have?"

The old man secured his other hand on the last of the four brandy
glasses, paused unnecessarily but to great effect, then fired down that
last brandy, actually spilling some across his chin, which seemed to
delight him and foreshadow what he belted out next.

"No Money!"

. . .

So … at least the old man knew what he "had," and drank accordingly. I was in the therapist's office about to hear a life-changing assessment. Hell, I wished I was at the bar of the Four Seasons to hear this.

She came in, introduced herself, and told me to sit down, which was foreboding as I was already seated. After a long pause, which was totally unnecessary, she spoke.

"Mister Steer, the reason your condition has taken such a long time to diagnose is because we had to rule out the obvious. We thought you have A.D.D. But you don't … You have A.D.D."

I said, "Please sit down," not noticing that she had already sat down next to me.

"I went through months and months of intensive therapy, and now you tell me I don't have something, but I do?"

Yes, she said… "it is something we have not seen before."

I said, "But I have not even traveled out of the country!"

"This is not an exotic affliction, but it is extreme," she said, not trying to calm my fears.

"Give it to me straight, Doc," I said bravely.

Any time you are saying "Give it to me straight, Doc" you know you are in trouble.

"Ok, well you are familiar with A.D.D. right?"

"I think so; it is a deficit of ability to pay attention. No?"

"Yes. Correct. Exactly. Juvenile minds sometimes succumb to this."

"Yes, yes, I see … wait! … so what's that got to do with me?"

"Mr. Steer … You have the first known case of a new kind of A.D.D. You are Patient Zero!"

A hush went across the room. Well, at least I was pretty quiet.

She said, "Your disorder is that you have a **deficit of attention paid to you!**"

I launched up from the couch! *"Yes! Yes! I DO!"*

As I was yelling yes, so was my therapist…

"We finally found you! You are Patient Zero!"

"I am I am!" I yelled!

"I've spent hours and hours on a couch telling you about me…

Now you are telling me about me …

Go on … Please go on!

It's working! Tell me more! I feel better! Please say more!"

Ok, so what do we have here? A delightful story and a play on words. Well, that is hitting the jackpot. Right?

So, I guess it would be important to tell why this story/tale exists in public rather than it just be a funny thought in my head. This whole "patient zero" story is meant (at least by me, you can do with it what you will) to be told in front of a woman that I would like the attention of. I know the way that sentence ended is bad grammar, but just follow me.

One could take the boring and perhaps ineffective path of telling the truth, the correct answer path. It might sound like this: "I hope that you will turn your attention to me and find something about me that makes you want to learn more ..." Well, good luck with that!

One could take another tempting path and that is to flat out lie. That might sound a bit like this: "I was just made partner of the firm and I am deciding between the Lambo or the Maserati." Again, good luck! How are you going to follow up that load of crap?

So, the story would not be told *to* her, but within her range of hearing. Hopefully, the fact that the story is about me having some unique malady, that I am sharing loudly in a crowded bar, draws her attention to either learn a reason to turn off her already triggered attention, or to watch me fall off the high wire. But the trick is on her when she watches while on the edge of her seat and realizes that the story was always meant to be just a private signal to her that we should pursue the chemistry that I believe is there, while the story made the crowd burst into laughter which showers me with the antidote to the A.D.D. that I have!

Again, let's run it through the Apparent Logic filter, but this story wears the answers to many of the questions on its sleeve.

Is the story the truth?

In the previous story about the way to hang toilet paper, I say the story is as good as the truth. It is a guess, but one that is not a stretch of the imagination to believe it.

Did the story hurt anyone? Of course not.

Did I gain at the expense of anyone? Nothing to gain from anyone.

Did the story move the intended person to move toward my thinking? Completely!

Did the story delight the others?

Were the words I used happy to come off the bench and get into the game?

Ahh, these last two questions are the key to this story being an example of Apparent Logic. Others are happy with the answer and the words themselves are happy to see the light of day, to be called into action, knowing the deliverer of those words could have easily passed on the opportunity since they were insufficiently prepared to give the correct answer.

Apparent Logic once again blazes the path between the boring truth and the hurtful lie.

CHAPTER XIV

A VOYAGE THROUGH THE UNFORCED ERRORS OF NAUTICAL NOMENCLATURE!

I f you give me a minute, I will give you a degree of understanding about Latitude.

Degrees and minutes ... hmmm.

Ever wonder why Latitude is measured in degrees, and then minutes? And then each degree of Latitude is then divided into sixty seconds. So, a unit of temperature is then divided by units of time. Got that? Good. Follow along.

The only way to explain is to put yourself on a sailing ship at the equator. Why a ship? Well ... because we are talking about measurements of the surface of the Earth, so we should not be high up in the Himalayan mountains, nor should we be in the depths of the Marianas Trench in our explanation. We should be on the surface ... at sea level. And I think we can learn from Sailors' experiences sailing the seas.

You don't notice on the surface of the earth as a pedestrian nor would you in an airplane where you really don't have a sense of distance. But you do on a ship. It is always right at sea level where the degrees and minutes are distributed. The horizon is pure at sea level.

So, the explorers and navigators back in the day needed a system to call out where you were on the planet. In two-dimensional terms that is easily solved with a grid, an evenly marked grid, just like in the game Battleship. See ... ships help explain things. One axis is letters, and the other is numbers. By the way, the one place to never put your battleship is on the coordinate B-4! It has to do with the fact that B-4 is actually a word; Before, so subconsciously everyone will think of B-4 and eventually yell it out! That's a story for another chapter I feel, so we will set that point aside.

But the grid goes all to hell when you place it on a sphere. However, the idea of a grid is hard to let go of, so they bastardized the grid into what they called Latitude, which they took plenty of, and Longitude, clearly because they wanted to make up a new word, which we applaud. With probably less forethought, they realized they needed units of measure for this new "grid" and just borrowed some units from real scientific disciplines to give this whole scheme an air of legitimacy and gravitas.

So, we now divide the major increments into "Degrees" and the minor increments into "Seconds." This all happened while the Thermo-scientific and the Chronological societies were recovering from hangovers after the big, first-ever scientific confab known as The World's Fair, held in London that year. A week later, they sobered up to find that their degrees and seconds had been ripped off by the Cartographers. When you think about it, with all the money offered by the Kings of England, Spain, and Portugal for the Cartographers to come up with this new mapping system, I'm surprised the Kings paid off for such shoddy and plagiarized work. Truth be told, which is actually not the purpose of this book, the new system of Latitude and Longitude, with its degrees and seconds ... was very effective. Sailors could now give directions to fellow sailors to reach certain places to plunder.

But ... they never foresaw the unintended consequence of their mapping scheme. They drew pretty globes with lines all over them, but they missed what would happen when you go from two dimensions to three. This unintended consequence is what we now know as the "Space/Time/Temperature Continuum." Let me explain.

There are 89 degrees between the Equator and the North Pole. They wanted 90 degrees, but the last one was just a dot on the North Pole. Once the Cartographer consortium decided on the 90-degree scale, they assigned the implementation of this gradation scheme to the Map Artists Guild. Artists work in Guilds. The Cartographer's work was done, so they left it to the Mapmaker artists and went on holiday.

They assumed the Mapping Artist Guild would have used their logic in where to start the degrees. Here was their logic: Degrees are a unit of measure for temperature. Back then, before a man made global warming, a 90 degree day was hot! If they created latitude today it would have to go up to 100 degrees. So, the 90th degree was meant to be the last degree of latitude, and that would be found at the equator. So, each next lesser degree would correspond to a drop in temperature as you sailed away from the equator. A brilliant use of heat measurement which created a redundant system for measuring distance. If your sextant reading was obscured by the clouds, your thermometer was your backup. Hidden in its name is the code for this device. Thermometer … *"Thermo"* from Latin meaning heat, and *"Meter"* from Latin meaning distance.

In the nice temperate range of 55 to 75 degrees of latitude from the Equator being at 90, one finds themselves in place like Chattanooga, Tennessee, and Hawaii, enjoying golf and tennis and sunbathing and farming. As you head further north, the degrees drop in the 35 to 55 degree range and you are in places like Salem, Oregon, enjoying hiking and spring skiing and snowshoeing. Soon you hit the Arctic Circle at 20 degrees, and you are in places like Greenland and you are not enjoying. You are miserable as you reseal windows and fix the sauna and stock the larder for more miserable cold nights ahead. It was left for Admiral Shackleton to place the 0th degree of latitude on the North Pole with his flag. His highly acclaimed account of that trip hides that fact that on his deathbed he was said to have said, "I wish I found the equator instead."

Just to support this argument that the degrees were meant to start at the North Pole and not the equator, the zero being placed at the North Pole would also signify that there is zero going on there. I mean zero, zip, nada. Zero belongs up there and not at the equator where women dance in grass skirts and rum was invented, probably in reverse order, but you get the point. These systems had hidden redundancy in them that wasn't hard to see.

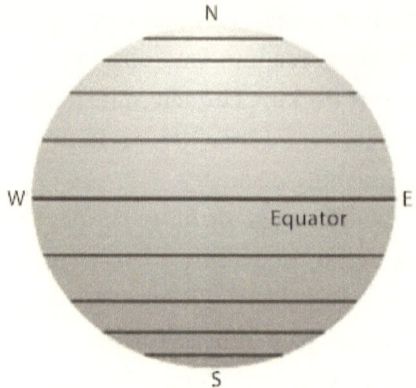

So, let's look at the globe now with the latitude drawn on the map. You can see the Map Artists Guild placed the latitude far apart from each other near the equator, and the latitude is increasingly closer together as you travel to the poles. Each degree of latitude has its 60 seconds in between, so that stays constant. So, as you sail from the equator, each degree covers a much longer distance than those degrees near the poles. That makes each of the 60 seconds slower.

Therefore, when you are up at the Arctic Circle, the distance to cover 60 seconds is much shorter, making each second quicker! A ship travels faster at the Arctic Circle than it does at the Equator! Again, The Space/Time/Temperature Continuum.

When the Cartographers sobered up and regathered to see what the Mapping Artist Guild had produced, they were extremely pleased at first sight of their genius scheme coming to fruition, but there was one major glitch. They had not given the logic to the map artists and so we now have the equator at 0 degrees instead of 90 degrees! No small error here, as that mistake contributed to the sinking of the Titanic years later!

How you say? Glad you asked ...

There was a good episode recently of History's Greatest Mysteries, with Laurence Fishburne, on the events that lead to Titanic's demise.

In short, the major factor in the sinking of Titanic was pilot error. The captain of the ship made mistakes. What was the single biggest mistake he made? Speeding! Or, as cops say, "Failure to leave a safe distance based on road conditions." Titanic was going too fast through an area filled with icebergs. Given that they were down to using a watchman to visually sight icebergs in bad weather, there couldn't be enough time to react. You can't turn, nor stop, a ship of her size without plenty of room. Other ships in the area had either stopped travel or slowed to a crawl in those conditions.

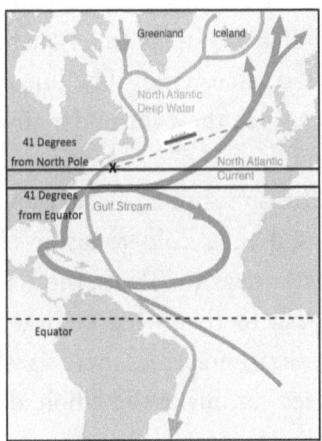

And ... where was Titanic on the globe at that ill-fated moment? She was at 41 degrees of Latitude. But which 41? If she was at 41 degrees from the Equator at 90 degrees, she would have been sailing right into the safety of the warmer Gulf Stream waters. But we know that wasn't the case. Put her at 41 degrees from the North Pole at 0 degrees, like they intended the maps to be drawn, and she is sailing right into the path of the conveyor-belt of icebergs ... the North Atlantic Deep-Water current coming down from the arctic.

Had maps been created correctly, with the degrees of latitude starting at zero on the North Pole, the Captain could have looked at his charts and seen how cold it was and how fast he was passing through minutes, then proceed with much more caution by slowing down to account for the Space/Time/Temperature Continuum, where ships go faster near the Poles than they do near the Equator.

This is also why sailors make a big deal about crossing the equator. They know how the degrees of Latitude were reversed and still honor the original intent. They called the degrees of latitude along the equator "Masters Degrees" as there was much to learn drifting aimlessly in the great expanse between degrees. They know it's time to find an island, find a woman, slow down, warm up, have some rum, smoke, music and dance, and generally take a vigorous moral inventory of your life in those slow minutes. Or you might even do something that may end quickly, but at the Equator that same activity would seemingly take a nice, enjoyably longer time. Sailors have known that secret ever since they got under those three sheets to the wind.

Sailors also know the opposite effect takes place close to the Poles and are reluctant to sail in a colder, faster climate. As your ship gobbles up minutes faster near the Poles, the act of sex can be over in the blink of an eye! Add to that what George Castanza pleaded in "Seinfeld," that in the extreme cold there is shrinkage, the sailors know that these realities can make the whole damn attempt more of an embarrassment than pleasure!

Now let's compound the linguistic errors committed on the bridge of the Titanic that fateful evening. In addition to going too fast in poor weather conditions, there is a rumor passed down in ports along the Atlantic about the verbal commands given by the captain. As Titanic was steaming from the north to the south along the upper eastern coast of the North Atlantic, she would have the ocean to her left and land to her right. (See diagram)

Fog and icebergs all around and a watchman in the dark up on the bow of the ship giving last-minute signals with his flags. As a huge iceberg appeared out of the fog on the right side of the ship. The watchman signaled the Captain for Titanic to steer left to avoid the iceberg. The captain's choice of words sealed the ship's fate when he yelled down to the engine room, "HARD TO PORT!!"

Port ... port already had a meaning when it was assigned the designation for a safe inlet along the coast to rest up and take refuge from a storm. So why the hell was it later assigned another meaning, which is the left side of the boat? Starboard being the right side. Hearing "Hard to Port" had the engine room put Titanic in a hard right turn, towards shore and the nearest port. Those good intentions, and the right front side of Titanic's hull, were smashed against the iceberg. In a bit of gallows humor, the rumor also includes the most junior members of the engine room crew, when abandoning ship, stopped by the captain's quarters to each steal from the captain's wine collection, hoping there would a bottle of his finest Port left remaining.

People who use the word "Port"

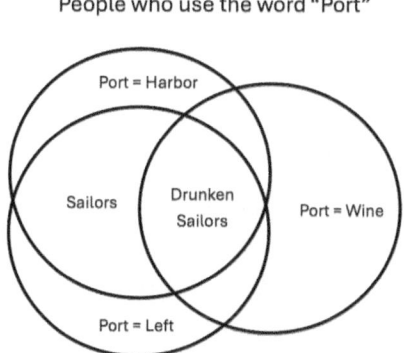

If one meaning was nautical, while another meaning was horticultural and a third meaning applied to numismatics ... well then, we would not have so many people lost at sea! But leave all three meanings in the realm of drunken sailors and, ... that's why I prefer to fish from the shore.

Right...?

Starboard!

Wait … what? Let's now give the other direction a bit of consideration. Apparently … left is not the only fubar direction. "Right" in nautical terms is starboard, right? Right! But what do we know about the word "starboard?" Glad you asked. What is a starboard? Well, it is a star board. Back in the early days of sailing ships that were a part of a formal navy, such as the English fleet, there was a need for all on board to recognize the highest-ranking officer on the ship at that time.

How did they do that? They displayed a bright white star on the board that correlated to the highest-ranking officer. A five-star Admiral was recognized with five white stars. Where did they display that? On a board. It was called the starboard. At first, the starboard was displayed across the outside of the stern of the ship to let everyone outside the ship know who was on board. Then after that proved to give enemies incentive to attack that ship to capture the high-ranking officer, it was moved to the inside transom of the ship to let the crew know who was on board. And so, the starboard was always known, directionally, to be the back of the boat. That was until another poor effort at well-chosen words resulted in the starboard forever meaning the right side of the boat.

Had they just stuck with right and left, we would have avoided hundreds of years of naval navigation verbal errors and so many shipwrecks. I don't think we even need to complicate matters any further with a review of "fore & aft," nor "stem to stern." I think we place our exclamation point on this part by paraphrasing the last line from the movie "King Kong," by saying …

"Oh no, it wasn't the icebergs.
It was words sunk the Titanic."

So, to wrap up here … Now you know a whole lot more about mapping, direction, time, and sex. Probably more than you wanted to know, so my job is done. But let me bring this whole thing home for you in a situation that you might encounter tomorrow.

Let's say you ask a person to take a moment for a chat, and that person, unbeknownst to you, is a sailor. You might use this phrase: "Hey, do you have a few minutes?" You will get an answer like: "Yeah, make 'em quick." That's because a sailor knows that some minutes are slow and some minutes are fast. He may say to make 'em quick because his degrees are cold and he is in need of port in a storm. Makes sense now that you know where quick minutes and slow degrees are found … doesn't it?

~

Remember a while back you saw a page in the front of this book, dedicating this work to those in pursuit of well-chosen words. Now you can see that effort is not merely just to hit heights of entertainment and profound messaging. It could be a life-or-death situation caused by a poor choice of words. I am not just talking about the person deciding which word to use. No, much blame needs to go back to whoever decided what a word is to mean!

"Port" for left for sailors.
"Degrees" for units of measurement.
"Minutes" for units of distance.
For God's sake!

We champion the use of words. We give glory to each one. We relish when a new word enters our lexicon, like Gamesmanship. When assigning a meaning to a word let's be a little more creative and make up a new word…not retread another meaning to a word already in use!

That is single-word plagiarism and lazy at its core!
Phew … where was I?

If you need inspiration to come up with new words, just visit your local IKEA store! Hell, they even make up words without vowels just for fun!

Back to judging this story as a beautiful example of Apparent Logic. So, to prove this story is not a lie, let's measure it on the unnecessary scale. A lie is necessary to keep a perception intact. This whole argument is just the opposite. It has very little purpose. Almost completely unnecessary. It only came about on a long car ride to trip up my

German engineer friend. Lies don't exist for sheer verbal sport and entertainment.

There is also a typo in this chapter ... or is it? There is a single letter placed or misplaced that offers two opposite positions, with one offering an inside joke, and we now know how powerful those can be.

Did I mean to say, "man-made global warming," or did I mean to say, "a man made global warming?" Did that "a" find its way on paper on purpose, or as an easy mistake to overlook? That's for you to decide. Without that "a" the point being made is backed up by the argument that human participation on our planet has contributed to global warming. That's easy to accept and therefore makes it easy to overlook the "a" as a typo that means nothing. But if you do not support the argument about humans causing global warming, then that little "a" offers a different take. Saying "a man made global warming" indicates that one man, a single person, made global warming. And who could that be but none other than Al Gore, with his slide show called "An Inconvenient Truth." I'd love to do the Finite Humor math to see what percent of the readers took the path with the inside joke. I admire a good play on words, and I sure hope there is an honorable mention for humorously twisting an argument with one letter!

We go from one letter out of place to a string of words that have an odd feeling to them. Only three consecutive words, but they might give you a sense of uneasiness as you read through them. The words are *"... Port left remaining."*

While they seem to exist without too much grammatical infraction in my sentence, save for a hint of redundancy, they accomplish a writing feat that I will lay claim to be the only writer to have achieved! That is ... until I stand corrected. These three words have this unique attribute:

The 1st word is a definition of the 2nd,
and the 2nd word is a definition of the 3rd!

I'd like linguists to give that a name, like there is for a palindrome. I've already created the phrase "Single word plagiarism." Could it be the written equivalent of being in a house of mirrors? Let's call it a "Triple Entendre," where a view from any one to the other gives a glimpse of all three.

Why does our language let an innocent bystander, using words, go astray so wildly? Why are there such verbal M. C. Escher drawings hidden in our language ready to trip us up and lead us down unintended staircases? As the practitioners of Apparent Logic, we don't need to know why. We just celebrate the chance to take what was given us, using every word, and every meaning of those words, to craft our stories that are better than the real answer.

Remember what Titus said in his testimonial for this book, or rather the testimonial that I wrote and attributed to Titus, which, by the way, doesn't make it any less true.

"The most important, yet unnecessary book of our time."

Others might take that as a slight, but not me. Think of the last time someone responded to a nice gesture you made by saying, "Awe ... you didn't have to do that." They were essentially saying that your kind gesture was unnecessary, but so appreciated. That's how I take Titus' comment, which I remind you, I wrote for him. So I love his appreciation, and will your's too.

I didn't have to write this book, but as a nice gesture to the world ... I did! Awe ...

I also think this Titanic story would make for a great episode of "Drunk History!"

CHAPTER XV

BEACH TOYS!

W hen I was a salesman I travelled the Tri-state area visiting supermarkets in New York, New Jersey and Connecticut to see that our bottled water was present and prominently displayed. One summer, on a visit to a Jersey shore independent market, I came across a wire bin filled with stuff kids need for the beach. The sign made that clear. There were beach toys in the wire bin. A shovel, a pale, a beach ball, etc. The sign said "Beach Toys." But it also said beach toys in Spanish, as such "Juguetes de playa." Something about that sign caught my attention.

Fifteen letters and two spaces in Spanish and nine letters and one space in English. 66% more letters, and twice as many spaces on the page.

No conclusion to jump to … just the observation. It stayed with me, filed away as an interesting observation.

Visually, it doesn't seem that much longer, but that is because of an optical illusion where the use of center justification hides the length difference. Look again …

Beach Toys
Juguetas de Playa

Versus

Beach Toys
Juguetas de Playa

The difference does not make one better or one inferior. Isn't having more better? And conversely, isn't using more than needed wasteful? Leave those questions behind at this point and just observe.

Back when I was that salesman and saw this sign, I told my observation to a friend at lunch and his reaction was at first "so what?" Then, since I pestered him with my early implications of this observation, he sort of dared for me to follow this line of thought. That was so long ago. The span of time between observation and action on this story is prolly the longest of them all. I saw him recently at a gathering of work alumnus and we went right back to the Spanish versus English observation. The dare for me to finish picked right up from where it left off long ago!

I wanted help gathering further observations, so I put a small team together of college students who were friends of my sons. My sons, seeing where this might go ... passed. One of the team was studying psychology, another anthropology, a third was a business major. A good mix of disciplines to undertake the needed field research. The psychology major noted a sign in a church that she encountered during Covid. That sign was on every other pew, closing them off for social distancing. The whole lockdown gave us time to make plenty of observations about life in general.

"Please do not sit here"
"Por favor no siéntase esta aquí"

The anthropology major noticed signs instructing us how to wash our hands and began forming a thesis about how we may not actually be moving forward as a species, but in reverse. I look forward to her finished thoughts being unleashed upon the world!

"Employees must thoroughly wash hands before returning to work"
"Los empleados deben lavarse bien las manos antes de regresar al trabajo"

As a funny aside, she also noticed written in pen on the bottom of the sign, this:

The business major, who read a lot of business books, looked to books for his observation. It was quite revealing. He had recently read Malcom Gladwell's *"Tipping Point"* on my strong recommendation. While I was looking at words and phrases for my observations, he took his observation much further, like to eleven, and purchased another copy of *"Tipping Point,"* this time in Spanish. I was happy to see his interest level high enough that he would invest his money to make his comparison … at the book level. He sent me this picture along with his observations:

Sure enough, there were significant findings:

English version had 272 pages
Spanish version had 324 pages

The Spanish version was 19 percent longer. And guess what? The business major was fascinated at a conundrum that goes against all he was learning about economics. The two books cost the same! Huh? That's a mystery. If the Spanish version came first, it would all make sense as insidious marketers have used the tactic of keeping price the same but lowering the quantity you get in the box. Sure, your favorite cookies are still $3.99; however, it is no longer 20 oz but rather 17.5 oz. You don't get more for the same price. Perhaps he will form another team to research that anomaly.

Now that we have made the observation that Spanish is longer in written form, we must ask, what are the implications of Spanish being 19 percent longer? One place to look for that answer is the market for printer ink. Ink toner sales are expected to hit thirty-seven billion dollars by 2025. If we were to use 19 percent fewer letters, then that is a seven-billion-dollar savings! That's significant. There would be less paper used as the number of spaces required would also be reduced. The market for copy paper is fifteen billion dollars. That is a bunch of trees saved … no? Hmmmm …

So now where do we find ourselves?
Entonces, ¿dónde nos encontramos?

We have followed observation and questioning through several rooms, and each time the answers have taken us in a new direction. Now we are in a fifth room level place. Meaning what we ask or observe next could not be seen unless traveling through those previous doors with judgement held aside. Our research has established the written Spanish language is, on average, significantly longer than English. We explored several ramifications of that observation.

So now what? Do you leave it at that? No. Not when your Apparent Logic story has built momentum. If you only have an ounce of curiosity within you, there is still a huge question which reveals itself in this fifth room. What question would you have?

"Is spoken Spanish longer than spoken English?"

I know what you're thinking. What dangerous rabbit hole are we rushing through now? Strap on your non-judgmental gear and let's find out! Apparent Logic has no ill intent, but it does have an abundance of curiosity.

Does it take longer to say something in Spanish than it does in English? And once we enter that sixth room, what observations will lead to further questions? To find out, we armed ourselves with stopwatches, clipboards, folding tables, and several common phrases printed on paper in both English and Spanish. Here's what we chose:

"Can you tell me where to find a good restaurant? I am new to this town."
"¿Puedes decirme dónde encontrar un buen restaurante? soy nuevo en esta ciudad"

"A life vest is located under or between your seats. To wear it, tear open the plastic package, remove the life vest, and slip it over your head."

"Hay un chaleco salvavidas ubicado debajo o entre los asientos. Para usarlo, abra el paquete de plástico, retire el chaleco salvavidas y deslícelo sobre su cabeza."

"The use of words separates us from the rest of the animals. Let's choose words carefully."
"El uso de las palabras nos diferencia del resto de animales. Elijamos las palabras con cuidado."

The first phrase was to disarm the participant by being a useful common phrase encountered in everyday life. It should come off in a non-hurried manner. The second one is also very familiar but has a sense of seriousness. It is meant to be conveyed with authority and perhaps haste. The third phrase is just profound and provocative. Maybe it is also a tip of our hand to let them know they are taking part in groundbreaking, yet meaningless research.

Thus armed, we hit the streets. We chose two different street corners in the east village of NYC and set up shop. Nothing screams legitimacy more than a folding table, clipboards, and stopwatches in the East Village of NYC. The consummate melting pot of New York, or perhaps it was consommé in that crackpot, I mean crockpot. Anyway, we were deliciously prepared to engage the public. We let the passersby choose if they wanted to speak the English or the Spanish phrase, not wanting to further offend anyone. We even tried, fruitlessly, to cull out certain samples from our data set where, as an example, a Hindu chose Spanish and took far too long to even say "Are you kidding me?"

There we were, stopwatch in hand. People were very happy to oblige us in this essential field research. Many just spoke the phrases as we timed them. Their tempo seemingly not hastened by the awkwardness of the situation. Those that read the phrases had friends looking for news crew cameras, but alas, it was just us. Occasionally, we would encounter a bi-lingual person. Actually, more than occasionally. We had to create a separate category for them so as not to corrupt the findings. Oh yeah … the findings …

Well, we recorded so many different times. The range of times for the English speakers was pretty wide. Imagine a Texan saying phrase 3 and compare that to a New Yorker saying the same thing. There was also variation in range for Spanish speakers to say the phrases in Spanish, but less so than with the English speakers.

Let's put aside the range and get to the heart of the matter. For the same phrase in both languages, it took a slight amount of time longer, 8 percent, for the Spanish speakers to say what was written. But do you remember that in the written languages the Spanish language requires 19 percent more ink and paper to express the same thought?

What does that mean? Doesn't every fiber of your curiosity demand that answer?

. . .

Is it possible that the Spanish speakers have learned to compensate for the requirement to digest and deliver more letters than English speakers do by hurrying up their spoken language?

Try to follow two Spanish-speaking women in an argument and you will understand! That can easily be found by watching Latin romance TV shows.

I know that it is easier for me to understand Spanish that is written, because I digest at my own pace, but to follow along with beautifully spoken Spanish that throws so many words at you per moment, well, that's hard.

So, let's remember the bi-lingual people sample in our data.

We didn't really anticipate that we would need a mathematical equation to settle it all, but we found one. Words per Second. The bilingual subset data revealed something fascinating. The bilinguals speaking Spanish crammed more words per second than did bilinguals speaking English, in a way to express the same phrase in almost the exact same time! Maybe the bilingual can hear in their heads both phrases being spoken and mash it verbally to the allotted time it is given. Maybe this can only be accomplished by accepting that Spanish-speaking cultures are way ahead of English speakers in terms of musical rhythm and tempo.

So, if that speeded up spoken language is really happening, is there an effect from that? Is there any medical difference in the Spanish speakers that correlates to the quicker metabolism of words? Is there a higher incidence of high blood pressure? What is the cost of that on the health system?

Fortunately for all, which is me, my student field researchers, and the general public, we did not pursue the research needed to document the potential health emergency we uncovered.

At the end of our experiments, we sent off our findings to the Institute for Apparent Logic and had a great debrief at the speakeasy on the other side of the British phone booth inside Crif Dogs. Hat tip to Anthony Bourdain for that culinary secret. Two of the students took a real interest in the topic. The anthropologist wanted to learn more about the evolution of languages. The business major was fascinated by the economic implications and planned to invest in an ink toner company. The third, the psychologist, had a different area of focus after these on-the-street exercises. She wanted to focus on the eccentric, the idiot savants, the windmill-slayers of the world. She thanked me for being her inspiration for this direction. I didn't really know how to take that backhanded compliment, but since it was more attention on me (and my A.D.D.), I was happy, nonetheless.

For any really sensitive people who took offense that the data chosen, or made up, supports the idea that Spanish is longer than English … let's tap the breaks a little bit, and ponder the sign on this door. Play the Eagle's Hotel California and realize that you can never leave, but you come to that realization just a tad bit quicker in Spanish.

As long as we are on the subject of assaulting a language, let's pay tribute to Teddy Roosevelt who, as President, came up with a list of 300 words that he created by shortening the spelling of those words. He even tried to legislate them into everyday use. He must have been intrigued with efficiency, as he wanted to eliminate the "ed" at the end of many words that indicate something happened in the past. So, for example, Kissed, became Kist. Wow! That saved two letters from a six-letter word. That's 33 percent reduction! Personally, I'm not sure you should be striving for brevity when kissing.

However, we need to make an important distinction about Teddy Roosevelt's assault on words. It was not an effort against the use of words, in fact, I am led to believe he was quite loquacious in his communications both spoken and written. No, it was only an aggressive attempt on the advancement of brevity of effort!

I stand with Teddy Roosevelt!
More words & fewer letters!

Did you see how I could have spelled out the word "and" but instead replaced a three-letter word with a single sign?

So, there is an argument to be made that Teddy Roosevelt is the *"Father of Texting"* as he foresaw the beauty in a shortened written language. I will submit this as my second story for the show "**Drunk History.**" In my opinion, the best modern-day example offered by the texting generation is the word "Prolly" to replace the clumsy "Probably." Seriously, when you say "probably" correctly, you sound like you are stuttering. There is no sense in shortening a word if you do not remove a syllable or two. "**Prolly**" rolls off the tongue with ease as if its existence was never in question and those that use the longer version are just heretics and rabble rousers.

Brevity being the soul of wit is fine, and with Alacrity being the soul of Apparent Logic, I applaud Teddy Roosevelt's attempt to make words faster! Hell, they did it to minutes, why not words!

The idea of replacing alphabets is crazy. If we were to take this logic to its apparent conclusion, (and I know you see what I did there) not only would we replace the written language of Spanish with its 27 letters, with English, but we could also replace the 26 letter English alphabet with the 12 letter alphabet of Rotakas, which is spoken in Papua, New Guinea! That is a 54 percent savings! Hell, I'm the one who shortens my brother's name from TJ to T! That's a 50 percent savings.

This story just shows how dangerous unbridled curiosity really is. Which, as a conclusion to this story, is a preposterous mistake. It is crazy because we would have to change the way children think and that is not a good idea. Children question with the purest of curiosity. Creative types are reminded later in life to *think like a child* in brainstorming exercises. The fact that simple observation and questioning can get you in trouble is at the heart of my brother TJ's testimonial for this book.

In his testimonial, which I wrote on his behalf since he passed away ten years ago, TJ brings this observation / questioning to its natural and absurd conclusion by stating:

*"This is a dangerous book. The Queen's English was never meant to be bastardized into such an assembly as is put forth by my brother in **Apparent Logic**. The existence of this book calls into question the very foundation of our education system and screams out the existential choice we now face: Really ... should everyone be taught to use words?"*

CHAPTER XVI

A PARTIAL LOOK AT THE CURRICULUM FROM THE INSTITUTE

I n Stephen Potter's *Gamesmanship,* he makes frequent reference
to "The Institute" where the Theory & Practice of Gamesmanship was studied, workshopped, and taught to the next generation of hopeful Gamesmen. You clearly envision the Institute as the
building on the previous page. Old and beautifully designed for
higher educational purposes, the walls themselves could tell of
underdog victories in games of darts, billiards, lawn tennis, golf, or
any other gaming contest with proper rules. Victories tilted in the
Gamesman's favor by some well honed ploy or gambit. When I first
read Gamesmanship, in between the laughs I made a promise to visit
The Institute if I were ever to travel to England. Having had several
golf trips over there I'm sure I was very close to The Institute but
somehow the actual visit eluded me.

Now, with the creation of The Institute for the Theory & Practice
of Apparent Logic, I feel somewhat forgiven, even if only forgiving
myself, which is good enough for me. I base this Institute out of
Connecticut, USA, so now you can experience higher education
wisdom both here and abroad.

Potter kept referring to what was learned in the hallowed halls of
The Institute for the Theory and Practice of Gamesmanship as ploys
or gambits. They were the tactics to be deployed on the field of
sporting battle to gain an edge over the opponents.

In the Institute for the Theory and Practice of Apparent Logic, our
tactics are more mischievous than devious. However, I do like that
they rise to the standard of being a ploy or gambit … just verbal ones.
The following is a not complete list of Apparent Logic ploys or
gambits. It will never be complete because at the Institute we are
constantly fine-tuning existing curriculum and adding material from
devotees in the field as Theory gets put into Practice. To borrow a
phrase from another Institute of higher learning, there are no degrees
given at the Institute as learning is lifelong and therefore never stops.

See if you now recognize some of these elements.

· · ·

Powerful Circle of Observation, Curiosity, and Questioning

This needs to be first as these are required skills to see and not just look, to listen and not just hear, to feel and not just touch. This powerful circle works best, perhaps even only works, in a non-judgmental manner. You can only see what is in the fourth room if your story has brought you through the third room, and past any judgements that might inhibit questioning.

I could have stopped thinking about how written Spanish is longer than written English upon the first observation of the "Beach Toys" sign, anticipating that it may tread on divisive land, but I didn't. I didn't because I was cloaked in non-judgmental curiosity. I wasn't led by intent that formed the next question. It is not like a prosecutor might build a case with a goal in mind. In fact, what comes to mind is wisdom shared by Ted Lasso to his players after experiencing a very tough loss. He said something like, *"Be a goldfish, they forget everything in 5 minutes."* This is the opposite of intentionally building a case. With non-judgmental amnesia, you can objectively look at your surroundings wherever your story has taken you and make new observations that lead to new questions if you remain curious.

Let me share one of the most exciting moments I had while writing this book. It was in writing the "Titanic" story. I hope as all of you craft your next story with Apparent Logic building blocks, that you have an adrenaline filled moment where your observation and questioning lead you from one room to the next and you only then realize there is another observation that can be a huge piece of your story. I added the Titanic portion of the story after first delivering the Latitude part of the story to my friend on the car ride. I may have been in the fifth room of the story by then and once Titanic was added, and only then, did I realize there could be an amazing fact that would provide the scaffolding for a very strong next part of the story. I remember reminding myself to look up what was the latitude where the Titanic struck the iceberg and sank. I was so excited because I was hoping, by sheer coincidence mixed with good luck, that it would be at 32 degrees latitude. I wanted that to be because I was correlating degrees of latitude with degrees of temperature and the story would have gushed out of my head about the water freezing at 32 degrees! The Captain's map would have told him there could be icebergs and the redundant system of the thermometer would have confirmed the map reading!

I was so disappointed to see that the sinking of Titanic was at 41 degrees, thus freezing out that whole part of the story. I pivoted the story to include the Gulf Stream warm waters and the inversion of the degrees of latitude starting from the North Pole to save this part of the story, and I like it, but I would have been so pleased to learn that Titanic sunk at 32 degrees. I say that with no disrespect to the Titanic families. I'm just telling a story about mapmaking with nothing to gain.

Hippocratic Oath

The comments above segue nicely to this next tenant of Apparent Logic, and that is, like the Hippocratic Oath that Doctors pledge, to "First, do no harm." It is a great check-in question for yourself as your observation and questioning during your story brings you to shaky ground. Stop and ask, "Was any harm done?" Remember that a lie damages the soul of the teller, and it harms the recipient as it steals truth in a way that deprives them of acting accordingly in their own interests. For those friends caught in the Apparent Logic of my Facebook post, coincidentally on April Fool's Day 2016, I hope you got a smile after realizing there is no such thing as "Up-tempo Gregorian Chants."

The Unnecessary Scale

Where is your story on the unnecessary scale? Remember, the words you chose for your story have likely not seen paper nor have they been verbally tossed in the air. They were chosen to bolster an argument that didn't have to be made. Wear the badge of unnecessariousness proudly. The fact that you gained very little, maybe even nothing, from the considerable effort you put into the argument should not deter you. No, in fact, let it be an important sign along a path, a rock cairn of sorts, that lets you know you are headed in the right direction. The words themselves appreciate that you chose them.

Imagine, if you will, that there is a coach of a team with many players. This coach is special. This is the word-choice coach in your head. Each of his players are a specific word. As the coach intercepts the intentions of the host in which he inhabits, he assigns players (words) to take the field of play. Those words will see real action as the coach puts them into play, at the behest of the host.

The coach knows all his players and looks for chances to get them on the field, but the path chosen by the host can be repetitive as the host chooses the correct answer. Once again, the same words are trotted out onto the field, words that are tired of their responsibility. The coach is yelling "C'mon lads! You done this before. You know exactly what to do. Just like in practice!" and other efforts of encouragement to inspire words that, while correct, are bored.

Less often, the coach intercepts the host's intentions of lying. The coach cringes. He regrets putting hurtful words onto the field. He knows that over time, those words, no matter the variety they take, will be followed by another repetitious string of apologetic words that sheepishly take the field. These words themselves are injured and injurious. It is not the type of on-field performance the coach relishes.

Now, very infrequently, but hopefully more frequent due to this book, the coach stands up! Is he getting the right reading from the host? The coach isn't sensing the need for tired old words to explain the truth once again. No ... no he is sensing something different in the intentions of the host and automatically the coach's sensors go off with deviation from the truth. As the coach puts the first several words into play, he notices that they have not seen action in quite a while. Then ... there it is! A phrasing is being requested by the host that is grandiose. Is it truth? Is it a lie? It doesn't seem to be either, judging from the reaction of the recipient of the words. Those words jumped onto the field and took their positions with vim and vigor and a hint of mischief!

The coach is running back and forth amongst his roster of words, diving deep into the bench where there were tons of words as fired up as the Hanson Brothers of Slapshot fame.

The coach screams *"Look! HE'S GOING APPARENT!"*
Finite! Get off your ass, you're going in!
*Theory! Get out there next to **Finite**!"*
***Amorphous! BeMorphous!** Where the hell are you guys?*
***Stop touching yourself!** Yeah, all of you warm up and get ready!*
From down the bench the word "**probably**" yelled out, *"Hey Coach ... am I going in?"*
The coach replies *"Yeah, **Prolly!**"*

The Power of Math

One of the earliest stories I wrote, for no apparent reason, was the Theory of Finite Humor. It is beautiful how math offers a way to explain the power of an inside joke. Remember, we are trying to bring the listener on an easy journey to the result. Math has solved way more important tasks than that, so it should be able to handle being used for a harmless justification here and there. The beauty about math is that it has rules, strict rules, so if you don't violate them, by saying 2+2 = 5, then you bring a pillar of credibility into your story. Yes, if ten people each get 10 percent of the humor, well, that is easy to understand. And if only five get it, they get the other people's 10 percent as well, which means those who got the joke each get 20 percent of the humor, or twice as much as if they all got it.

None of that violates math. So, it must be true then ... right?

And when you don't actually have "the exact number," well then, at least we all know it exists. Since we know it exists, then we all have some educated guess what it might be. Therefore ... a believable number in the right ballpark is as good as the correct number. Know the unknown. If you don't have the correct stat handy, insert yours. BeMourphus Soccer is filled with placeholder stats. The story doesn't hinge on whether it was a 26 percent chance of happening, versus a 28 percent chance. After all, everything can be boiled down to a 50 - 50 chance of happening. Either it does or it doesn't.

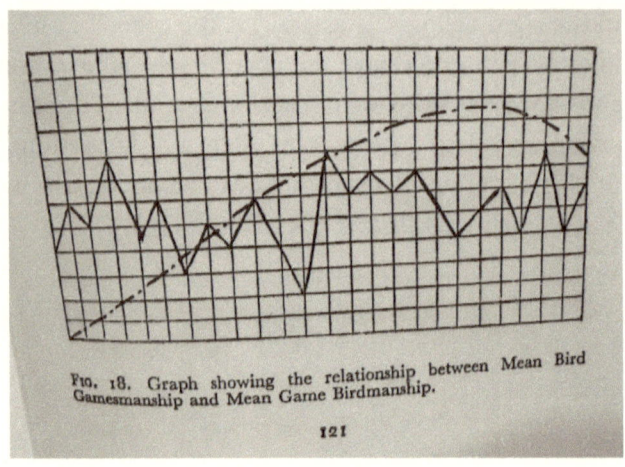

121

This is Steven Potter's graph showing the relationship between *"Mean Bird Gamesmanship and Mean Game Birdmanship."* Before dissecting the graph, let's try to understand it. What is Birdmanship? Well, it is a subset of Gamesmanship, which is the art of winning games without actually cheating. So, think of Birdmanship as the ploys and gambits that would make you look more knowledgeable about the subject than an Ornithologist. Especially if the expert is accompanied by an attractive female you want to impress. An example may be while on a jaunt in the woods, to ask the expert if he too just saw the elusive Frog Pippet fly by. Only you know this is a made-up bird name, so the expert is left flustered in front of his date. A time proven gambit.

But in this graph, Potter examines how far from math you can go and still gives the air of legitimacy created by invoking the semblance of math. I love this graph because it has the audacity to not even be a graph! There is no X or Y axis labeled, so the lines may not be relevant data at all. The graph itself may likely just be a tracing of the silhouette of a mountain range or a sample of someone's EKG. But when coupled with a description that has no meaning, well … it stands as a genius example of Apparent Logic.

. . .

146

The Power of Quotes

Just as math adds the air of legitimacy to an Apparent Logic story, so to do quotes. Quotation marks around a quote signifies to the reader that someone else said something, hopefully relevant to the story being told. As we know, a good Apparent Logic story has the listener engaged in much hesitation and confusion, trying to follow along with what the storyteller is saying. That builds up a bit of suspicion by the listener about the storyteller such that when a quote is offered, the listener will gladly accept words from someone other than the storyteller. The quote rescues the listener and in so doing, what is said by the person being quoted is accepted with less scrutiny, giving a much-needed boost of credence to the overall story. Who could ever forget the memorable lines from the following non-existent situations?

The Doctor in "The Other A.D.D."
The Director in "Written, Spoken, Heard"
The Kids in "Greatest Graffiti Ever"
The Coach and Players in "BeMorphus Soccer"

Let me add a subset to the "Power of Quotes" by highlighting the power of quotation marks themselves. It is not just attributing what is said by using quotation marks that gets elevated in importance. A name for something can gain increased importance by bookending that name in quotes. Is there really such a thing as "Impulse Singularity?" Has that name emanated from extensive peer-reviewed scientific studies, as the quotation marks seem to imply? Or … is it conjured up from my imagination as apparent logic stage decorations being hung on the tantalizingly close scaffolding of truth? While we are at the task of answering that question, we might as well throw in a related question about proper grammar. Do I need to use quotation marks if it was me who said it in the first place?

. . .

The Voluminous Detail

Sometimes a good Apparent Logic story is a shortcut that gets a person to the intended place of mind quicker than the truth or correct explanation. Perhaps the Toilet Paper story, or the other kind of A.D.D. story, might fit that description. But often you just get neck deep describing loads and loads of details so that the story must be true to the listener because they can actually "see" it. The Greatest Graffiti is such a story. One of the first people to have read that story, which appeared in my first book, had only this to say, "Did that really happen?"

There is a magnificent story told in the movie, *"The Usual Suspects."* The whole movie is the story, carefully and recklessly weaved together by Kevin Spacey's character, coincidently named Verbal. Verbal is brought in by the police detective, who is trying to unravel a case involving murder, theft, and deceit. Verbal is this harmless-looking character who, each time he is brought in to explain his inno-cence and answer questions, he spins more story. A story filled with such detail that it can't be not true. The story includes a menacing, ferocious criminal who Verbal blames for all the mayhem. That scary mastermind, according to Verbal, of course, has a scary and exotic name ... Keyser Soze! Men will commit suicide rather than have Keyser Soze on their trail. Keyser Soze is never seen and is almost mythical, but his threats are carried to their intended victims by his right-hand man named Kobiashi.

Since The Usual Suspects has been out awhile, and since it is crucial to linking Keyser Soze's story to the gambit of 'Voluminous Detail,' I think it is ok to reveal that Verbal Kint made up the Kobiashi name by seeing the brand name on the bottom of the porcelain coffee cup the detective had, every time he raised it to his lips. It was a Kobi-ashi coffee cup! In fact, most details of Verbal Kint's alibi used names he saw on the bulletin board behind the detective. The detective only realizes the whole story was made up after he lets Verbal go for good, and sits in Verbal's interrogation chair, looking back across the Detec-tive's desk. The Detective then sees all the names and details of Verbal's alibi on pages pinned to his bulletin board and the icing on the cake is that in shock, he drops his coffee cup ... it breaks on his desk … the Detective looks down and sees the crucial puzzle piece to the story … Kobiashi!

The Kobiashi / Keyser Soze story was the alibi of a thousand details. Highly recommend that movie, Kevin Spacey's finest role.

The 5th Level Detail

The kids who wrote "Our Names" were listening to Violent Femmes … really? And it was the song "Blister in the Sun?" Really?

This story could easily have gone from the kids getting together, right on over to the act of spraying the graffiti, with zero requirement to explain further. But why shortcut the story and miss a chance to add layers of detail? So, instead, I added an answer to the question, "What were the kids doing at the time?" Check out these layers that have no real purpose except to create a more vivid picture of the events.

What were they doing?
Level 1: Hanging out in the basement
Level 2: Sizing up their chances with the opposite sex
Level 3: Playing music
Level 4: Listening to Violent Femmes
Level 5: The song was "Blister in the Sun"

Minute detail such that it renders all other explanations … including the truth, useless due to boredom. A person would be disappointed with the truth once they hear the Apparent Logic version.

. . .

The Recognizable Red Herring

This is meant to establish a new believable beachhead to pull the reader/listener away from the previous less-believable shaky ground. The World's Fair, Andy Kaufman, the soccer logo.

It is the garden stake that allows the meandering tomato plant to achieve heights it has no hope of attaining if not for the straight, upward scaffolding upon which to hang. It's the truth from which apparent logic gains credence.

Alacrity is Your Friend!

If Brevity is the soul of wit, then Alacrity is the soul of Apparent Logic. By the time they cycle through the "Yes! Wait … What? You are already on to the next part of the story!

Wayne Gretzky explained his strategy in hockey. He said he would skate to where the puck is going to be. You are the verbal Gretzky, having left where the audience is digesting the last words and creating the new words they need to move towards.

Every Interaction is a Chance

As a practitioner of the Theory of Apparent Logic, our loyalty is to the words themselves. Why is a ridiculous explanation like the Theory of Finite Humor even necessary? Excellent question. It is our duty to put words on the playing field of life, words that would otherwise not have seen the light of day. Make those words happy to be chosen by choosing them. Don't wait forever for the perfect moment. My brother TJ lived his life with the notion that every interaction with a stranger was a chance … a chance to mess with them! He often viewed everyday situations as a stage. This, by the way, is the same man that flew F-14 Tomcats off aircraft carriers at night. He had plenty to keep him preoccupied with rational thought but … yet he, too, found time to engage in the arena of ideas! His were just a bit sporting at times.

Case in point. A long time ago I was walking down Main Street in

Rye, NY, with TJ, on our way to Poppy's café to revive ourselves. We came upon a crowd gathered around a car that had ended up on the sidewalk some time earlier. It was police-taped off and other than its presence where it was not supposed to be, it was a day like any other. Joining the assembled rubberneckers, we stopped and looked at the car. Without any indication that he was going to engage the crowd, he said loudly, *"Somebody should do something!"* The perfect pairing of urgency and vagueness. It was so delightfully uncomfortable. While his words were perfect, I can't go further without the highest praise for the delivery. It was not said quietly to me by his side. It was not said with any hint of questioning in the tone. No, it was proclaimed. If you are telling people where the fire exit is while the building is burning, you proclaim it. It was delivered as if it were handed to each person, like a subpoena. Now it was fully in their hands. In their heads. It was up to each person to decide how to act, now that action was called for. But due to the absolute vagueness, the people could have fulfilled TJ's proclamation by simply lighting a cigarette. It was then time for us to leave and continue our walk to Poppy's Café, where I spit my coffee all over myself, laughing.

Forgo the safety of your local pub with your best friends. Get out on the front lines! At the neighbor's barbeque, or at the veterinarian's office, offer an opening line ... a preposterous opening line, that invites the assembled people to follow along. There are exits all along the way, but I bet they stay for the verbal journey as you climb the scaffolding and bring them with you! Finally, to the end, where they are now gifted with your kind gesture, and they are left wishing they had that time back, and with a desire to inflict the same kind of verbal effluence on the next person.

And thus, the institute of Apparent Logic, and the legions of practitioners, grows...

FINAL THOUGHTS...

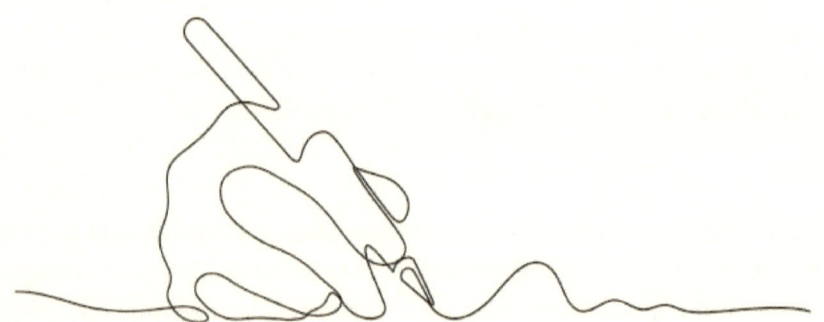

As an esteemed author, I am often looked upon for literary wisdom. Such was the case when a thirteen year-old boy walked forward in the Apparent Logic book-signing line with his Dad and posed a poignant and profound question. His question, coming from such an unknowing, youthful age, was so at the heart of what we are trying to do here, which I remind you is to use well-chosen words. Well, his question actually stumped me. But only for a moment.

He asked: *"What is your favorite word?"*
Boom! He hit me out of the blue with a literary haymaker! So many to choose from!

I could have told him the truth … that I didn't have one.
I could have lied to the young lad and said "Megalodon" or "Boisterous" or "Shoe-box!"
There is something about the two syllables, the hyphen, and that it sounds like it describes something more significant that what you put baby birds in that fall out of the nest.
I could have digressed, in order to buy time to think, by telling my least favorite word, which is "Pandemic." I mean, who didn't love hearing instead "An epidemic of global proportion?"
Remember, we are trying to put words into use that have been sitting on the bench waiting for the chance. More words. Not less.

No, I chose the Apparent Logic route because I knew that at least one of us would love it.

"You know, Kid, my favorite word is "Counter-intuitive." I have always liked that word and have always wanted to use it in a sentence. You'd think that would be easy, but in fact, it's not. Look at this book. It took to the last page to find a way to use my favorite word, "Counter-intuitive." You think it would be easy, but it is just the opposite of what you think. Hmmm … there's a word for that, but it just doesn't come to mind right now."

That little wordplay has flown over the heads of much taller people, including the kid's Dad. The smile and the knowing look from the kid made me believe that both of us enjoyed that unnecessary but rewarding conversation.

Apparent Logic was in good form that day, with our interaction enlisting a future talent in The Theory and Practice of Apparent Logic.

You may be wondering if this story is the Truth.
Or, if it is a Lie.

Does it hurt anyone if it is not true? No.
Then, as we have learned, it is not a Lie.

Did it really happen?
Well, did it get you to believe it happened? Yes.
Then it can only be the Truth ... or Apparent Logic.

I should leave it at that.
But I can't.

There is an observation you could make ...
How could a story of a book signing be included
in that book being signed?

Welcome, my friends, to...
The Institute for the Theory & Practice of Apparent Logic!

www.ingramcontent.com/pod-product-compliance
Lightning Source LLC
Chambersburg PA
CBHW050404110726
47899CB00008B/2650